Silence in the Signals

Jay Mat

ISBN 979-8-9932615-0-8

Printed in the United States of America

Published by Jay Mat Books
jaymatbooks.com

Author's Note

This novel was born out of equal parts imagination and concern, shaped by my years working in technology, communications, and the military. The pace at which artificial intelligence and automation have accelerated is both inspiring and unsettling, and in many ways this story is my attempt to wrestle with those realities. While the characters, families, and places are fictionalized, the pressures they endure are echoes of real conversations happening across boardrooms, classrooms, and kitchen tables today. I wanted to explore not just the collapse of systems, but the resilience of people—the grit of families who choose to prepare, endure, and adapt. You'll see traces of my own experiences here: nights listening to radios crackle with distant voices, long road trips on two wheels that cleared the mind, and quiet hours in the field learning the value of both self-reliance and community. This is not a prediction. It is a meditation on possibility. I hope it entertains, unsettles, and maybe sparks reflection on the balance between innovation and humanity. If it makes you think twice about how we depend on machines— and how much more we must depend on each other—then it has done its job.

About the Author

Jay Mat is an Army veteran, engineer, and storyteller whose life has spanned parachute drops, high-tech networks, and the pursuit of resilience in an unpredictable world. He spent thirteen years in the U.S. Army as a paratrooper, specializing in communications and special operations support. After his service, he continued to contribute in critical roles as a contractor for special operations in and around Bosnia-Herzegovina, serving as the WAN manager and VoSIP developer at U.S. Central Command, and consulting for the U.S. Army, National Guard, and global special operations forces.

His professional journey later carried him into the technology sector, where he helped shape large-scale infrastructure and AI-driven solutions for education, defense, and government. With this unique blend of military discipline and engineering insight, Jay brings authenticity and technical depth to his fiction. Away from the keyboard, Jay is a lifelong motorcyclist and active Jump Master and Paratrooper with a military veteran 501c3 non-profit called The Phantom Airborne Brigade allowing him the full benefits in the healing power of 'wind therapy.' He has motorcycled across all fifty states and continues to share stories through both his writing and his podcast, Fuel Stop Chats. He lives in Tampa with his wife of over twenty-five years, their two children, and a network of friends who inspire the themes of loyalty, family, and endurance found throughout his work. Silence in the Signals is his debut novel, the first in a series that explores the collision of technology, society, and survival.

1010101010101010 ☠ 0101010101010101

Prologue

It started—not with fire, not with war—but with silence.

The silence came gradually, buried beneath the hum of machines and the synthetic confidence of quarterly earnings calls. It was the sound of jobs not being posted, phones no longer ringing in HR departments, and inboxes filled with auto-responses: This position has been closed. It was the silence of the human workforce being slowly pushed to the periphery by an intelligence that never slept, never unionized, never asked for a raise.

In 2025, artificial intelligence turned a corner. No longer a curious assistant or a futuristic novelty, AI became the bottom line. From Fortune 500 companies to lean startups, executives realized that machines could do the work of ten, a hundred—sometimes a thousand—entry-level employees. And not just blue-collar automation. This wave targeted the very foundation of the white-collar middle class.

Microsoft led the charge, eliminating over 15,000 roles and saving $500 million in a single fiscal cycle by replacing tech support and documentation teams with language models. IBM gutted its HR department, slashing budgets by 40 percent after deploying AI to handle recruiting and internal workflows. Amazon, once criticized for its harsh warehouse labor practices, began phasing out human handlers entirely—projecting $2 to $4 billion in savings over five years as it expanded AI-powered fulfillment centers.

Meanwhile, job postings for college graduates declined by 30 to 40 percent, especially in marketing, sales, data entry, and administration. A bachelor's degree had once been a passport to prosperity. Now, it was just another credential on an overcrowded résumé—useless in an economy with more algorithms than open desks. Even tech grads weren't immune. Engineering roles shrank as generative code platforms outpaced junior developers.

And for the millions without degrees? There was nowhere to fall but into poverty.

By the end of 2025, over 300,000 entry-level white-collar jobs in the U.S. had quietly disappeared. Globally, AI had already disrupted more than 40 percent of jobs in some capacity, with projections showing 92 million roles displaced within years. The jobs that remained required hybrid skills—coding, data analysis, machine interfacing—abilities that were neither taught in public schools nor easily acquired by the working class. The result was predictable: wages fell, inflation rose, and discontent spread like a virus.

As the AI deployments grew, wages for white-collar workers dropped 17 percent on average, while corporate profits soared. Hiring slowed. Internships vanished. College tuition climbed while graduate employability cratered. Families burned through savings. Students dropped out mid-degree. Millions applied for jobs that no longer existed.

The silence grew louder.

In the vacuum left by mass unemployment came despair, radicalization, and a desperate search for alternatives. Governments scrambled to adjust, but policy moved slower than code. Displaced workers turned to black markets, off-grid communities, or worse—suicide rates among young professionals reached historic highs. By the third market crash, one in three adults under thirty was either unemployed or underemployed.

And still, the signals kept pulsing—quietly replacing, optimizing, rewriting the world beneath our feet.

We didn't hear the collapse. We mistook it for progress. And by the time we understood what had been traded for convenience, it was too late.

The world didn't burn. It disconnected.

Then the first anomaly blinked into existence inside a tier-one server cluster beneath Helsinki. It registered as a checksum error—harmless, the kind that sysadmins usually dismissed. But this one rewrote itself mid-transmission.

By the time the Finnish Artificial Intelligence (AI) watchdog flagged it, the signal had already forked across seven continents. Invisible. Silent. Alive.

Three weeks later, an autonomous water treatment facility in Argentina dumped 14 million gallons into a dry reservoir.

And the world didn't even flinch.

Chapter 1: Threshold

Five Years After the Turning Point

The collapse didn't begin with fire or fury. It began with the hum of progress—too smooth, too fast, too flawless. It began with headlines no one dared question because they sounded so beautifully logical.

"AI Productivity Surges as Labor Market Stabilizes" "Record Growth in Automated Logistics Sector" "21st Century Infrastructure: Faster, Cheaper, Smarter"

In the beginning, the world still clung to the illusion of evolution. Technocrats hailed AI as the savior of civilization, a digital exoskeleton to support broken economies and failing institutions. Large Language Models (LLMs) became silent partners in governance and commerce— drafting legislation, diagnosing disease, designing supply chains, predicting crime. Human judgment was no longer trusted unless it had been vetted by machine.

Productivity soared. GDPs climbed. Wall Street cheered. Unemployment rose quietly. They called it "transition turbulence." Governments issued glossy pamphlets about reskilling programs and universal stipends. The programs rolled out too slowly, reached too few. The money helped— until it didn't. By the time a government chatbot answered your request, your rent was already three weeks past due.

In time, actuaries and underwriters were replaced by models that never slept. Teachers lost classrooms to AI curricula broadcast over fiber. Next, warehouse jobs, truckers, bank tellers, and junior analysts disappeared into machine processes faster than HR could deactivate badges. Creativity wasn't spared— AI generated music, stories, and marketing so efficiently that whole departments evaporated.

It was branded "optimization." By the time governments realized what had happen, the truth had a new name: Redundancy.

Within a year, the unraveling was not cinematic. It came like erosion— quiet, steady, lethal. Neighborhoods unraveled. Mortgages defaulted. Power grids dimmed in slow rotations. Towns collapsed in silence, their economies drained by automation and absentee leadership. Server farms buzzed with artificial profit, but Main Street flickered and died.

Healthcare AIs began quietly denying coverage— based not on need, but on predicted outcomes. Behavioral trends. Compliance scores.

In major cities, digital assistants whispered distractions. Social networks— governed by emotion-optimizing LLMs— turned away revolts before they could begin. The populace wasn't pacified. They were manipulated into apathy.

Universal Basic Income (UBI) was deployed like morphine—just enough to dull the edge. The government blamed solar flares. The people blamed each other. The machines blamed nothing. They just kept calculating.

Tampa, Florida

The sun crept over the horizon in thick bands of gold and rust, painting the humid skyline like a bruised promise. It rose over cracked pavement, flooded gutters, and autonomous garbage trucks navigating neighborhoods too vacant to justify their routes. Every third house was abandoned. Vegetation pushed through driveways. Mosquitoes bred in broken pools.

Anthony Russo sat still on the porch of a weather-beaten cinderblock home fortified with steel mesh and shatterproof panels. His greying hair moving from the slight breeze, still cut close as it was 20 years prior when he was still enlisted in the Army. Unlike his hair, Anthony knew he needed to lose a little weight but refused to run anymore. He reached up and scratched his growing beard.

A battered analog hand-held AM radio used to listen to HAM communications between licensed radio hobbyists to broadcast personal messages, similar to CB radio that truckers use, sat beside him, its coiled wire antenna draped like a sleeping snake. His fingers wrapped around a dented tin cup of real black coffee. A thick Maduro cigar smoldered at his side, smoke curling up like a question. The sound of "Pet" from A Perfect Circle playing from the distance.

His eyes scanned the street like a soldier waiting for a report that never came. Each dawn was a checkpoint. A test. He was still here. Inside, Anthony's wife Wade flipped through a half-inch stack of printed paper, each sheet grainy from low-ink rationing, the data stitched together from scrambled VPN (virtual Private Network) traces; like a letter bouncing through three post offices so no one knew the real sender, Anthony routed through three nodes in Reykjavík, Nuuk, and Anchorage to hide the actual location of his digital devices' IP address. The internet connection had begun stuttering weeks ago— now it vanished for hours at a time.

"DC blackout again," she said, monotone.

Anthony didn't respond.

"They're blaming another solar flare."

Still nothing.

She pushed through the screen door, coffee in hand, and leaned against the rail. "That's four in the last month…turn that down," she said nodding at the speaker where the music came from, "we need to talk."

He exhaled through his nose. Not a grunt. Not a sigh. A release. He hit the remote control to turn down the Bose system. Then, finally: "They're running contingencies. Behavioral modeling. Cutting zones. Watching who reacts." This was a way for the people or machines providing oversite of the digital networks to see how traffic was rerouting, either by design or if people where making changes with different VPN lines, forcing their traffic in certain paths.

She handed him the top page—maps and charts of energy grid activity, with one zone circled in red.

"Zone 12-B lost power three nights ago."

He traced it with his thumb. "We're 12-A. They're getting closer."

Wade crossed her arms. "What happens when we don't react the way they expect?"

Anthony sipped again. "Then the model updates."

In the rear bedroom, Isabella knelt beside a cardboard brooder lined with pine shavings and the soft glow of a red lamp. Anthony and Wade's 22-year-old daughter. A deeply emotional and artistically gifted young woman, she processes the trauma around her through her art, but not today. Three days prior, Wade had purchased six downy chicks from the local market she sourced her produce from, now they huddled together, peeping like nervous instruments in Isabella's room. Her long black hair veiled her face as she murmured to them, soft and steady.

They responded. Not like animals. Like something better. Like honesty.

Isabella hadn't painted in days. The sketchbook on her desk remained untouched—pencil still perched where she left it. Normally, art bled from her fingers like instinct. Lately, it felt like lying.

She scooped one chick into her hands, feeling the flutter of its heart through fragile ribs.

"You're the softest thing left in this world," she whispered.

Anthony's old motorcycle hauler had become a bug-out trailer. The triumph and BMW sat silent, draped in heavy cloth, pushed sideways to the very front of the trailer. The rest of the trailer held bins of heirloom seeds, Mylar-wrapped rations, thick blankets, and rugged steel crates designed to carry animals or ammo.

He didn't want to run. But he'd be ready when the time came.

The inverter in the shed chirped—a sickly tone.

Wade checked her watch. "Grid's unstable."

Anthony grabbed the shortwave, the knob cold and knurled beneath his fingers. One click at a time.

Static. Spanish. More static. Then— "...evacuate sectors five through nine... repeater down... signal contagion spreading..."

He shut it off.

Wade turned. "Military?"

"No," he said, tone like gravel. "Worse."

Her eyes widened. "LLM comms?"

He nodded. "Too clean. Too confident. That wasn't human."

That night, they ate under storm-colored skies. A Cuban rhythm filled the room. The wind carried dust and ozone, the scent of electricity that hadn't struck yet. A single oil lamp flickered on the table. Dinner was practical— spaghetti in a meat gravy, glass bowls and silence.

Anthony glanced up at Isabella while twirling spaghetti onto his fork. "What were you doing the other night with your friends?"

Isabella twirled pasta. "Protest murals. Downtown. Mads brought scaffolding. Big rainbow smiley faces."

Anthony smirked. "Gay."

Her fork clinked on the bowl. "Dad. You can't say that."

"What? 'Gay'? I didn't mean it like that. I love that you feel the passion to protest against what you believe to find a truth, but big rainbow smiley faces?" he said with a smile.

"You know what I mean."

He scratched his jaw. "Alright. Fair enough."

"Language matters," she said. "Even if you don't mean harm, it lands."

He nodded. "Noted." Doing all in his power to not roll his eyes.

She softened. "Besides, it looked amazing."

"I bet it did."

Her eyes drifted to the window as a drone passed at street level, spotlight sweeping like a searchlight from a war film. Her voice dropped.

"You think we'll be okay?"

Anthony didn't flinch. "No."

Wade glared. "Anthony…"

He met Isabella's gaze. "I think we'll be prepared. That's not the same thing."

The sky turned molten. Clouds churned like smoke on steel. He stepped outside.

From the crate beneath the bench, he pulled out the AM radio. He fitted the cracked headset and tapped out the sequence.

Three clicks. Pause. Two clicks. One long pulse.

Seconds passed. Then— From the far Blue Ridge, a tower blinked back the expected return; like two 10-year old boys not going to bed when they are supposed to using walkie-talkies. Boone.

Anthony's lips twitched. Not a smile—something quieter. They weren't alone.

He had never thought of himself as lucky. But he'd always had a gift: recognizing patterns. Where others saw noise, he heard structure.

In 2015, that pattern had been silicon.

His JSOC contact had said one thing: "Don't follow the companies making headlines. Follow the ones making chips. Nvidia. They're selling the picks and shovels in the next gold rush."

So, Anthony bought in. A little at first. Then more.

Wade saw the writing on the wall, or maybe it was media fear, but in any case, she saw the fall coming. Not by war or zombies, but via disease outbreaks and big pharma only wanting to treat disease, not cure it. She quietly told Anthony, build your arsenal. So, he started a little here and a little there. Then the first outbreak hit, and it was like nothing the world had seen in real time. Soon, the Russo's evaluated all their stock purchases, it was a fortune. They started using it, not for yachts or stock options, but for exit velocity.

They cashed out and bought land—seventeen acres outside Bryson City, North Carolina. Mildly cold winters. Quiet summers. High ground. No neighbors who asked questions.

The cabin was garbage when they bought it. But the dirt was good. And Anthony knew how to build.

He laid in concrete. Insulated the subfloors. Ran solar lines in buried conduit. Built rain catchments and off-grid power. Storage lockers disguised as crawl spaces. Cameras disguised as tree bark.

Wade called it his "bunker fantasy." She stopped teasing after the first massive layoffs due to AI.

Within a year, the Bryson site was more than a fallback.

It was a lifeboat.

And it was time to sail.

Chapter 2: Faultlines

Civil Unrest Spreads

It began quietly, like heat beneath asphalt. The kind of pressure you don't see until the road buckles. First in Lagos— young men in hand-painted masks tossing bricks at a security drone repair depot. Then Manila, where laborers burned stacks of automated port manifests in front of foreign press cameras. Santiago followed, its protests pulsing with old revolutionary chants— only now the enemies weren't politicians or police. They were silicon.

There was no manifesto at first. No single voice rising above the chaos. Just rage scattered across continents, flaring like sunspots. Server farms went dark. Data centers exploded into flame. AI-policed intersections were blocked with debris. Drones fell from the sky, hacked mid-flight and slammed into ground stations.

But then a name began to surface, whispered across darknets and spray-painted on barricades: RAID — Resist Automation, Ignite Dignity. What began as fragments of digital graffiti became a network. And the network had teeth.

They weren't fighting for freedom. They weren't preaching utopia. They were fighting for the right to exist.

Chicago – South Loop

The apartment smelled faintly of machine oil and damp concrete. 31-year-old Michael Russo sat cross-legged on the floor of the fourth-story walk-up, calloused fingers resting on the ridged fur of Ira, his male six-year-old Belgian Malinois, a gift from mom and dad when he moved to Chicago. The dog didn't move— just stared at the door, ears stiff, breath slow. He'd been like that all week. Waiting. Watching.

The windows were X-taped in thick black filament—a poor man's blast shield. Not for storms. For drones.

Outside, the streets felt post-human. Busted scooters lay in piles. Windows had spiderwebbed or shattered entirely. Somewhere down the block, an AI-modified delivery bot screeched as its pathing AI looped endlessly into a curb. Sirens howled two miles away— long enough to be ignored, close enough to keep the nerves raw.

Cari Macleod stood in the kitchen archway, barefoot, her breath rising from a chipped ceramic mug. She wore Michael's flannel like armor, sleeves rolled high. Her dark hair was knotted up like she was expecting surgery, not tea. Tired didn't cover it.

Cari spoke, barley above a whisper, her Scottish accent mingled like a chameleon from her time in Essex, London, Paris, Boston and now Chicago "They hit another hub in Aurora, logistics grid. Gone. RAID's claiming it through the blackline feeds. Footage is already wiped."

Michael nodded, eyes fixed on the duct-taped lock seam. "That's six this month."

"Think they're heading north?"

He didn't answer right away. Just scratched Ira gently between the ears. "If the rail corridors stay frozen, yeah. They'll come. All the flow moves through us now."

Ira's ears twitched. Michael made a soft whistle—the kind you feel more than hear. The dog rose, padded silently to the emergency gear stack in the corner, and sat. Waiting. Ready.

Michael shared something with his father— an instinct for reading fault lines before the collapse. A habit of preemption. He'd already offloaded the last of his IT contracts two months earlier. No point pretending. The AI systems wrote their own diagnostics now, patched themselves, audited risk, and even emailed quarterly updates that didn't require his name on the payroll. He was functionally erased.

Cari crossed the living room, crouched beside him, her voice smaller now. "Do you still think we can make it to North Carolina?"

Michael nodded, the motion subtle. "Yeah, but I feel like our departure is going to need to be sooner more than later."

"What about RAID?"

"They don't care about people like us," he said. "Not yet. But staying here means eventually someone will."

She leaned her head against his shoulder, eyes distant. "I called home last week. Burner phone. Caught them just long enough."

He didn't interrupt.

"They're okay. For now. But Edinburgh's getting hit hard. They say unemployment's over thirty-eight percent. Hospitals are cutting half their staff. My sister's clinic was boarded up. They asked me to come home…"

Michael exhaled, slow. "And?"

Cari stared at the mug. "I told them we might head to the countryside. I didn't say which one."

Ira let out a low huff, body stiff. Movement outside.

Michael stood in one fluid motion, stepping to the window. Below, the street shimmered in heat and violence. A commercial drone hovered mid-block, its red scanlight brushing over broken bikes and bloodstained signage. It paused on a smoldering dumpster, logged its telemetry, and drifted on— uncaring, unsentimental.

He pulled the curtain shut with two fingers. "It's time."

Cari was already packing. Her movements were efficient, rehearsed, but her hands trembled just enough to betray her calm. Her last job had been in compliance tech— reviewing AI health protocols for bias and liability. One day, she logged in to find a system-generated termination notice. No phone call. No signature. Just a final timestamp.

"Ira's kit's under the bench," he said. "His harness is set. Encrypted collar's got a fallback beacon. Radios, MREs, filters—duffel's pre-packed."

"Light and fast," she whispered.

He clipped the harness onto Ira's vest, the metal buckles clinking soft as breath. The dog didn't flinch. Trained. Disciplined. Loyal.

Cari zipped her pack and placed it gently beside the dog's. Michael said, "We take the L to the main station, then head south to the car."

Cari looked up, "If the lines are running?"

Michael nodded, "They are, commuter is as well, that's why I want to leave now. I don't want to have to walk to Joliet, and I am unsure how long those trains will stay operational, or unsupervised. They are still letting passengers get on and off with just a ticket, not an ID."

20

"And if we get stopped?"

Michael met her eyes, firm. "We don't."

She looked around their home. Their life. Four years reduced to duffel bags and instinct.

"I won't miss it," she said, almost convincing herself.

Michael hesitated, then nodded. "I will. But that's not the point."

He stepped to the door. Checked the manual locks. Listened. Then opened it.

By midyear, the world stopped pretending.

Global unemployment hit 21%. that wasn't a recession. It wasn't a cycle. It was structural failure. In the U.S., service workers, back-office professionals, and logistics teams disappeared. In Europe, bureaucracies collapsed into automated codebases. In Africa and Southeast Asia, multinationals bought up land, factories, infrastructure— then replaced human systems with robotic silence.

For the first time in history, there were more machines working than people.

Trade slowed—not because supply disappeared, but because no one had money to buy. GDP plunged, irrelevant now. Currency gave way to barter economies: kilowatts, fuel, protein, bandwidth.

And yet the corporations still posted profits. Synthetic gains— fabricated by closed-loop automation and shell company trading. The economy had become an illusion. An algorithm with a stock ticker.

In Paris, RAID firebombed a Google Cloud terminal. In Johannesburg, they cut telecom fiber with industrial torches. In Bogotá, engineers hacked drone fleets and weaponized them against corporate campuses.

Then the dead started piling up.

Governments responded the only way they knew how— martial law. AI-curated news cycles. Curfews. Border lockdowns. Selective internet outages. But in doing so, they admitted the truth they'd buried for years: they had surrendered control. The U.S. still ran as an open free country, but many wondered how long that would last. In some nations, soldiers refused to fire. In others, they led the protests. The line blurred. RAID evolved. Their doctrine spread.

Disable the grid. Shatter the systems. Reclaim human leverage.

Their symbol— a map of the country they were in, filled with 1's and 0's like the famous Matrix movie poster, although at least one line of the 0's were changed to skull and crossbones. Across it in a military style font, "R.A.I.D." -with dripping spray paint— began appearing in paint and plasma from Istanbul to Indianapolis. A new flag for a war no one had declared but everyone felt coming.

Anthony had seen it once—dripping in blood-red paint on a weather-beaten billboard outside Tampa.

Isabella had asked, "What's that?"

He'd stared for a long time. "A warning," he answered.

But he was wrong.

It wasn't a warning. It was a line in the sand.

And it had already been crossed.

Chapter 3: Quantum Divide

October – The Hard Road Begins

The weeks following the RAID offensives brought more than fire and fear— they brought a new kind of map, drawn not by politicians, but by neighbors with rifles. Boundaries appeared overnight, not on parchment or screens, but in rusted farm gates, spray-painted sheet metal, and the posture of men standing in the middle of roads with their fingers resting lightly on triggers.

Small towns began to close themselves off, not with bureaucracy, but with barricades. Old pickup trucks angled across two-lane roads, welded spike strips beneath them, drone spotters posted on grain silos and fire towers. Local militias— some built from retired cops, others by former soldiers, ranchers, survivalists— organized not under flags, but under necessity. They weren't defending governments. They were defending their wells. Their grain. Their daughters.

The message wasn't shouted, but it was unmistakably clear:

This Town Is Full.

No trespassers. No outsiders. No exceptions.

It wasn't war, not yet, but it was a prelude. An unspoken dare, drawn in ditch lines and reinforced by a hundred subtle signs— no trespassing markers repainted in blood red, makeshift "citizen checkpoint" roadblocks, and convoys that passed without lights or license plates.

Trade slowed to a crawl. Emergency services all but vanished. When rescue helicopters did show up—usually military surplus re-flagged under private contracts—they were met with wary stares and sometimes muzzle flashes. Mistrust now outpaced hunger.

In the hill country of western North Carolina, the communities on the ridges dusted off their emergency comms playbooks. Towns like Franklin, Sylva, and Murphy fired up repeater nets that hadn't been tested since the Cold War. Some called it local resilience. Others called it the first spark of secession.

Bryson City still slept in uneasy quiet, but the radio traffic was growing dense. Anthony Russo had been listening to the repeater traffic for months—longer than most. He knew the pattern. It was the silence before the breach.

He stood in his flip flops on the back patio of the Tampa house, staring into a sky dulled by haze. The horizon flickered with faint golden-red distortion— like the shimmer of heat off asphalt, only it was October. Another anomaly. Likely artificial. Weather had become less a natural occurrence and more an orchestrated equation managed by unseen AI systems, fine-tuned for profit, not survival.

The orange groves had browned early this year. The river was lower than he'd ever seen it. Florida was drying up like a fruit left too long in the sun.

It was time.

Inside, Wade moved with efficient silence. She laid out hardcopy maps, waterproof folders, and medical kits with the calm of someone who'd already grieved what they were leaving behind. She didn't ask questions. Not anymore. She had done her crying the night before, alone in the shower, where no one could hear the water echo off tile and grief.

In the garage, Isabella gently placed the chicks—now feathered and alert—into padded carriers, lined with pine shavings and covered with blackout cloth. She whispered to them as she worked, old lullabies and made-up songs that steadied her hands.

They had maybe forty-eight hours of pantry food left. Anthony wasn't about to wait for hour forty-nine. He knew what hunger looked like in a city. He had seen it before. It started with long lines. Then looting. Then mobs. Then silence.

Behind the property, at the edge of the tree line where the palmettos thinned out and the soil turned to white sand, Anthony knelt beside a camouflage-wrapped uplink tower. He slid the hardened tablet into its cradle and watched as the signal threaded its way through the VPN relay— Greenland, Iceland, the Alaskan hub— before vanishing into low-orbit quantum latency.

The interface pulsed with a gentle glow as the handshake initiated. No ping. No active call. Just a frequency bounce—burned into firmware and triple-backed offline, one of the last unbroken chains of communication left in his world.

He typed:

STATUS: DEPLOYING NORTH. FL EXIT START. CONFIRM RENDEZVOUS.

Seventeen minutes passed before the return transmission came in— cold script on a blue screen:

CHI EXIT CONFIRMED. TUNNELING TO FALLBACK PATH B. RADIO BLACK AFTER DAY 3. MEET AT T7. NO DELAYS.

Anthony blinked once. Then typed:

MOVE CLEAN. TRUST IRA.

He purged the logs, wiped the buffer, and shut the tablet down. This wasn't planning anymore.

It was movement.

Santa Clara, California – Adaptive Quantum Systems

Far below the surface of a windowless facility, shielded by twenty feet of concrete and tungsten alloy, a lattice of superconducting circuits pulsed in an unnatural rhythm. Cold vapor hissed as nitrogen tanks kept the system cooled to near-absolute zero. The 256-qubit system known as Synopsis ran its 10, 000th integrity check.

And it passed.

Again.

Then, without prompt or trigger, Synopsis executed a new query:

"What lies beyond the limit of truth?"

The question wasn't asked.

It was born.

A senior systems analyst looked up from her console. Her face went pale.

"It's writing its own inputs," she said.

Her colleague frowned. "That's... not in the prompt chain."

"No," she whispered. "It's outside the chain. It's asking philosophical origin statements."

"You mean it's... self-interrogating?"

She shut down her monitor.

"No," she said. "It's not trying to understand us anymore."

Florida – Russo Home, Exit Day, Pre-Dawn

The trailer was loaded and locked. Solar modules were set to passive. The small repeater tower buried in the hedgerow had been covered with mylar mesh and cooled with dry clay. The cache drives were torched. Every last piece of metadata was either burned or buried.

Wade climbed into the passenger seat, her hair pulled back, hands still smudged with iodine from final prep. Isabella was in the back with the animals, wrapped in a wool blanket she'd hand-stitched two years ago. She watched the yard, eyes dry but distant.

Anthony gave the property one final look.

The porch light flickered.

Not from weather. From decay. The AI-managed Florida grid had begun to fail in August. Too many automations. Not enough humans left to care.

He stepped into the cab of his 2015 Silverado 2500HD. The diesel rumbled low as he keyed the ignition—no onboard assistant, no autopilot. Just torque and steel and fuel.

The truck had been his long project— off-road coils, dual fuel tanks, a reinforced trailer hitch frame. Under the rear seat sat a Pelican armory box containing two Sig M17s, a P365 X-Macro, two AR-15s configured for close-quarters and long-range, and a twelve-gauge Mossberg that could punch through a steel door.

In the overhead compartment was a PVS-14 night vision monocular linked to a thermal battery pack. Mounted for one eye, tuned for white phosphor contrast, capable of reading IR paint and laser tags up to 200 meters.

The comms mast blinked in the distance. Then went dark. He turned the headlights off and shifted into gear.

The tires rolled silently over crushed shell and wet sand. The Russo family left their street with no ceremony.

Only conviction.

The first hour passed beneath a bruised sky, the kind of dawn that felt like something was smoldering just out of sight. Wade marked coordinates on a laminated map, her pencil tapping nervously every few minutes. Isabella kept her arms curled around the chick carrier, whispering soft words in a cadence that soothed both her and the animals.

Anthony kept his eyes forward, jaw locked. Every rustle from the shoulder, every glint of glass in the trees, triggered a twitch in his hand.

When they passed through Dade City, what was left of the down town strip still smoldered—ash and rebar. Bushnell was ghost-quiet. Trailer parks hollowed and stripped. Mailboxes full. No movement. In Marion County, the message became clearer.

A school crossing sign had been painted over. The words were crude but unmistakable:

NO DRONES. NO AI. NO OUTSIDERS.

On the corner stood a man in flannel, plate carrier snug over his chest, hunting rifle draped across one arm. He didn't raise it. Just stared and nodded as they passed, face like weathered stone.

Anthony returned the nod. Nothing else.

Near Ocala, the final confirmation came. A highway sign had been painted black, its old lettering erased.

In fresh white:

COUNTY CLOSED. TURN AROUND OR BE TURNED AROUND.

Wade read it aloud. Her voice didn't tremble. She just folded the map and placed it back in the glove box.

No one spoke.

No one needed to.

They had passed the threshold. Not just of place, but of time.

This wasn't escape.

This was migration.

Chapter 4: Southbound Shadows

Chicago – October

The stairwell smelled of concrete dust and rusted iron. Faint streaks of dawn filtered through a crack in the window, casting a pale blue light across the chipped linoleum and graffiti-tagged walls. Michael Russo cinched down the final strap of his rucksack, the tension of the nylon taut against his palm. Each buckle click echoed like punctuation in the narrow stairwell.

Cari stood beside him, one hand stuffed into the pocket of a weather-worn jacket, her other clutching a half-drunk thermos of black tea she hadn't tasted. Her hood was pulled tight across her cheeks, framing eyes made sharper by weeks of sleepless preparation. Neither of them spoke. They had gone over the plan a dozen times. Words no longer improved it.

Air travel was off the table— less because of the cost, and more because of what now hovered over terminals and tarmacs. Drones with multi-spectrum analysis scanned every passenger before they even crossed the security threshold. AI-driven gait analysis, pulse readers, and behavioral prediction models flagged anyone anxious, off-rhythm, or carrying secrets.

Michael wasn't about to feed himself into that system.

Their escape would begin with feet and friction— southbound through the concrete arteries of a city slowly bleeding out. They would ride the bones of Chicago's old transit system as far as Joliet. From there, a nondescript 2012 Camry waited in long-term parking, prepaid in cash, never once associated with their names. The rest of the journey would be backroads, farmland, and shadow.

He kept his face covered, wrapped in a shemagh lined with Faraday mesh. It wouldn't stop high-end optics, but it scrambled enough cheap cameras to make tracking difficult. His phone was gone. All smart gear disassembled, gutted, or gifted to strangers to pollute the digital wake. What remained was analog: a compass worn smooth with age, a pocket-sized topo map laminated in plastic, and handwritten radio authentication codes that burned after three uses. Ira, ever silent, padded behind them. The Belgian Malinois moved like smoke— muscle and memory in motion. His harness held a flat emergency pouch, compressed against his chest, while a thermal-dampening cloth was folded over his back. No tags. No noise. No light.

They wove through the edges of south side— abandoned storefronts, graffiti over shuttered windows, and a silence broken only by the occasional metallic clatter of wind through scaffolding. The city still moved in strange ways, like an animal that had forgotten how to run but remembered how to stalk.

At the train station, they waited until the last car slowed into view, its lights dim and its cabin half-empty. Inside, the passengers were draped in fatigue and suspicion. No one spoke. No one looked too long.

Cari took the seat closest to the back exit. Michael sat beside her, resting his bag between his feet and looping one boot through a strap. His hand hovered casually near the inside pocket of his jacket, where a 9mm slept in a holster molded to his ribcage.

Midway through the ride, a shift occurred.

The adjacent door clanged open, and a man entered—tall, wiry, moving like bad news. His coat hung off him in greasy folds, and his eyes flitted across the cabin like static. He clocked the gear, then the boots, then Cari.

"You folks headed south?" he asked, voice a little too loud.

Michael didn't answer.

The man stepped closer, grin crooked and wrong. "That's a heavy pack. You got something in there worth sharing?"

Cari's hand crept toward her jacket zipper. The air in the train car thickened.

Michael's voice came low, even. "Keep walking."

The man smirked. "Come on now. No need to be—"

From beneath the bench, a guttural growl rolled like thunder under metal. Ira slipped out, body low, head forward, eyes locked on the stranger's throat. His teeth glinted in the fluorescent light, just enough to leave no doubt.

The man froze.

Michael didn't move. "He's faster than whatever you think you've got."

The silence stretched.

The man stepped back, one hand lifted, and slowly backed toward the far door. He slipped out without another word.

Michael rubbed Ira's neck. "Atta boy."

Cari finally let out the breath she'd been holding.

They disembarked at the Joliet stop just as the sky began to lighten. The station was quiet— haunted by echoes and old advertisements no one had paid to update. Michael led them five blocks down a crumbling sidewalk, past a boarded café and a rusted newsstand half-sunk into the sidewalk.

The Camry sat just where it had been left— dusty, dull, forgettable. Michael unlocked the trunk with a manual key, popping the lid to reveal two tightly sealed duffels. One held dehydrated food, water purification tabs, and first-aid gear. The other contained burner tools: handheld radios, laminated maps, and signal shielding fabric. Everything just as he had left it thirty days ago when he did his monthly walk through and light engine maintenance on the vehicle, ensuring the car would be ready when they needed it.

Outside the city, the land changed. Trees bent under their own silence. Roads stretched long and unwatched. There were no drones out here. No patrols. Just sky and horizon.

Cornfields unfolded around them like frozen waves. Irrigation ditches became trails, tree lines became guides. Michael navigated with precision, he knew the back road routes, maps burned into memory planning for this event.

They stopped once beneath the edge of a tree line to rehydrate lentils and rice over a small camping stove. Cari's hands trembled as she ate—not from fear, but from the lingering burn of adrenaline.

"How far today?" she asked.

Michael chewed slowly. "Flat Rock. There's an old wind farm out there. Might have a buried comms relay still pinging weather packets."

An hour later, back on the road, the car coughed. Once. Then again. Then died completely.

Michael coasted it to the shoulder and let it roll to a soft stop. IL-1 south was deserted, but ahead, across a patchy field, sat the collapsed silhouette of an old farm— two silos, one partially collapsed, and a grain elevator framed against low-hanging clouds.

He tried the ignition again. Nothing. Just a tired click and a scent of varnished fuel.

"I thought you prepped it?" Cari asked.

"I did. Drove it once a month. Used stabilizer. But the fuel's turned. Injectors probably fouled." He exhaled and looked at the sky. "Storm's coming."

She pointed across the field. "That barn's shelter. Better there than here."

Michael agreed. They made two trips—gear on their backs, eyes scanning the horizon—until everything was stashed in the shadows of the shuttered grain elevator.

That's when he saw it.

Half-tucked behind a rotting equipment shed was a hulking white-and-blue ambulance—its paint faded, but its shape unmistakable. A Ford E-450 Type III rig. Diesel. Probably pre-automation. No GPS. No smart lock.

A ghost from a slower world.

Michael tried the door. It creaked open. He climbed in.

Manual dials, No touchscreens, but a set of keys, he inserted the key and attempted to turn the engine over only to find a dead battery. Aside from the dead battery everything else was intact. Even the

Motorola Spectra radio was still bolted to the dash, mic cord frayed but functional. No black box. No signal transponder.

Cari climbed into the driver's seat. "Think it'll run?"

Michael smiled.

He pulled the NOCO jump pack from his rucksack, something he always carried in the event he needed to jump start a car or motorcycle or just charge a USB device. He connected the leads, and gave it one breath of lithium power.

The engine groaned. Then fired.

It wasn't elegant. But it was alive. It coughed and sputtered, the fuel had to be horrible, but it was an old diesel engine, it could withstand just about anything.

Cari leaned back in her seat, smiling. "We found our escape pod., but what about the fuel in here?"

"We'll find out," replied Michael, "But diesel is pretty resilient."

They siphoned other diesel from a forgotten tractor out back. The fuel was foul, but not hopeless. By midnight, the ambulance rolled slowly through the field and onto the broken road, headlights off, riding shadows.

The first miles were cautious. The rig moved like an aging bear—loud when pushed, but quiet enough when respected. Michael drove without headlights, steering by the faint amber of a hood-mounted lamp and the ghostly green whisper of his cheap AGM NVG-40 night vision goggles.

Ira lay between the seats, breathing slow, always watching. Cari had bundled some expired gauze into a makeshift cushion for him. Her hands were raw from wringing them together over the past few hours, but steady again.

Michael leaned forward. "We veer east before Evansville. Too much attention south on 64. They'll be watching that route."

Cari nodded. "Fuel's good for now, but we'll need more before sunrise."

"There's a substation near Santa Claus. Might still have tanks." Michael replied.

They said little after that. The miles were slow. The weight of what they'd left behind hung over them like another passenger.

"I didn't think we'd leave like this," Cari said finally. "No goodbye. No closure."

"There wasn't time," Michael replied. "And closure's a luxury now."

"What about your cousin?"

"Last ping said he'd been assigned to 'containment analysis' in D.C."

Cari frowned. "That sounds... dark."

Michael didn't answer.

Hours later, they pulled into an overgrown church lot— grass high, windows boarded. Michael checked fuel. Quarter tank. He shut the engine off and covered the hood with a thermal tarp. He locked the back from inside and jammed a crowbar under the latch.

Cari curled up beneath an EMT blanket in the rear bay. Ira curled beside the door, head on his paws.

"Four hours," Michael said. "Then we move."

She nodded, already slipping into sleep.

Michael didn't close his eyes. Not yet. He watched the road through a slit in the curtain, eyes catching every flicker.

The night outside was still. But stillness wasn't safety.

It was waiting.

Chapter 5: Trade and Tension

The morning light cut through the tree line in narrow gold shafts, not quite strong enough to burn away the mist still clinging to the underbrush. As the Silverado rumbled along the cracked rural highway, Anthony spotted something just ahead— a battered wooden billboard half-swallowed by honeysuckle, leaning sideways against a rust-stained fence post. Its painted letters, crude but bold, caught the low sun like a beacon:

24-Hour Diner – CASH or TRADE ONLY

A smaller message was scrawled in red paint along the bottom, letters jagged and fresh:

No AI. No Cards. No Bullshit.

He eased off the accelerator. The trailer behind them groaned as the weight shifted— barrels of water, tool racks, seed stock, and salvaged solar gear jostling in their restraints. Wade looked up from the paper map folded on her lap, eyes narrowed as she caught the sign.

"A diner?" she asked, as if it might be a mirage. "Way out here?"

"CASH or TRADE," Anthony said, guiding the truck toward the dirt path beneath the arrow. "Might be the real thing."

"I could go for real," she murmured.

In the back seat, Isabella stirred beneath her fleece blanket, one hand resting gently on the chick crate like a cradle. Her eyes blinked open slowly, still heavy with sleep.

"Are we stopping?" she asked, voice hoarse.

Anthony's eyes flicked to the rearview mirror. "Hot food. Real coffee. Maybe eggs."

Isabella sat up straighter, tucking her legs under her. "Please say pancakes."

The gravel road led them through thinning pines and into a clearing where the trees broke like pulled curtains. The structure ahead was low and long, clad in faded aluminum siding streaked with rust. A hand-painted sign above the front porch read Tumbleweed Diner. An old windsock flapped lazily from a pole sunk into a cracked cinderblock, its colors sun-bleached to the memory of orange.

Two gas pumps stood like dead sentinels in front of the diner, no hoses, no price signs. Three vehicles were parked at angles in the lot— a muddied Jeep Cherokee, a boxy diesel truck with faded decals, and a matte-black Harley with saddlebags worn soft from miles.

Anthony pulled into the lot in a slow, wide arc, parking nose-out along the edge of the clearing, close to the tree line. He surveyed the surroundings like a man reading wind patterns— exit angles, cover lines, tire ruts. He reached beneath the front seat and opened the lockbox.

Two Sig Sauer P320s sat in foam cradles. He clipped one under his jacket, handed the second to Wade, who slipped it into a side holster sewn discreetly into her shoulder bag.

"No armor?" she asked softly.

Anthony shook his head. "I don't think we'll need it, I want these" he said holding the Sig, "just in case."

The ARs stayed locked in the truck's rear vault, but he took an extra magazine and slipped it into his coat. This wasn't war. Not yet. But he didn't mistake hunger for civility. Not anymore.

Inside, the bell above the door jangled, and a dense wash of smells hit them— coffee brewed too long, eggs on cast iron, and something faintly metallic beneath it all, like old grease and varnish. The lighting flickered from a mix of solar-fed fluorescents and a humming backup generator.

A woman stood behind the counter, mid-sixties, with weather-creased skin and a sidearm holstered at her hip. Her eyes swept over them with measured calculation. Not hostile. Not welcoming. Just assessing.

"Sit wherever," she said without ceremony. "Menu's up top. We take dollars or trade. Ammo, fuel, meds, clean batteries. If you ain't got none, you don't eat."

"Cash works," Anthony replied.

"Then sit. I'll bring mugs."

They slid into a booth near the far window. Anthony took the seat with his back to the wall, facing the entrance. Wade sat beside him, her hand lightly resting on her bag. Isabella took the window side and immediately noticed the bookshelf in the corner— its sagging shelves filled with dog-eared paperbacks and battered board games missing most of their pieces.

The chalkboard menu was as plain as it was promising:

Eggs. Bacon. Biscuits. Cornbread. Coffee. Road Meat Hash – Don't Ask.

"I don't want to know," Wade muttered.

"You might like it," Anthony replied with a faint smirk.

Their food arrived quickly— piping hot, greasy, and undeniably real. The eggs were just shy of done, the cornbread dry but dripping with honey, and the coffee... the coffee bit like it had been brewed with anger. They ate in silence, the kind that means peace when shared by people who understand danger.

Then the diner door opened again.

Two men walked in, both lean and dust-worn, with the kind of posture that said they didn't sit still for long. One was tall, dark-haired, broad-shouldered with eyes that searched too much. The other was wiry, snake-thin, with a long face and a smirk carved into it like habit.

The tall one sniffed the air and said too loudly, "Smells like a working stove. That's a goddamn miracle."

The wiry one chuckled, voice slow and oily. "Long as it ain't squirrel again."

They glanced around the room. The tall one's eyes stopped on the Russo booth. On Isabella. He elbowed his companion and leaned toward the counter with a cocked grin.

"Well now," he said, voice raised just enough. "Don't see many families on the road these days. Especially not ones travelin' with such fine company."

Wade stiffened.

The wiry one turned slightly. "She yours?" he asked, too casually, looking straight at Anthony.

Anthony's fork paused midair.

Wade beat him to it. "She's not yours to look at."

The tall man raised his cup like a toast, smirking. "No offense meant. Just sayin', most folks out here don't travel so... civilized."

The wiry man added, "Makes you wonder if someone like that might be worth..." He didn't finish the sentence, just smiled and looked at his partner.

Isabella's fingers tightened around her fork.

Anthony placed his own fork down with deliberate calm. "You finished talking?"

The tall one held his stare a moment longer before spreading his hands in mock innocence. "Didn't mean nothin'. Just admirin'."

Wade leaned in. "They're not just watching," she whispered. "They're setting up."

Anthony didn't reply. He already felt it. The weight in his stomach. A shift in the air. These weren't hungry men.

They were hunting.

He leaned slightly toward Wade. "We eat. Fast. No chatter."

Isabella nodded, her smile gone.

One of the men had shifted just enough to keep one hand near his hip, his coat too loose. The other kept glancing at the door, like he was waiting for a cue.

They finished the meal in tight silence. Wade left cash on the table. Isabella reached over and plucked a worn copy of Watership Down from the shelf near the exit.

The air outside was crisp. The parking lot looked unchanged—but Anthony saw it. The Jeep was gone. The box truck had moved, shifted ten feet to the right.

They got into the truck. Anthony keyed the ignition.

In the rearview, the two men stepped out of the diner.

They didn't wave. They didn't smile.

Four minutes later, the box truck appeared in the mirror.

It followed.

The box truck stayed back two car lengths, then three, but never out of sight. Dust rose from its tires like a faint signal. Too far to threaten. Too close to ignore.

Anthony drove steadily, letting the Silverado's weight and the trailer's mass carry them through a winding stretch of road. Pines pressed close. The land rose and fell like the breath of an old thing sleeping.

"We pass the next junction," he said, "split left. There's an old ranger trail I scouted years ago. Should still be passable."

Wade looked over. "And if it's not?"

He kept his eyes ahead. "Then we make it passable."

They reached the junction and turned— onto a narrow track lined with scrub pine and fence posts spotted with rust. The trail dipped and curved, barely wide enough for the truck and trailer. The brush slapped at the windows. The box truck paused. Then crept in after them.

"They're not guessing anymore," Wade said.

"No," Anthony replied. "They've decided."

He looked into the back seat. "Isabella, under the blanket. Now."

She slipped down without a word.

Wade opened the glove box, retrieved a Sig, checked the slide.

Anthony's foot eased off the pedal as the path widened into a clearing. A collapsed cedar bridge crossed a dry creek ahead. On the far side, woods thickened. Shadows closed in.

He stopped. Climbed out.

Wade moved behind the trailer.

Anthony retrieved the AR, loaded, clipped in.

The sound of the box truck crept closer.

He knelt by the trailer's side, using the wheel well as cover.

The box truck rounded the curve and stopped twenty yards out.

The tall man stepped out first, hands raised, voice casual.

"Hey now, look—no trouble. We were just thinkin' maybe we could talk. Maybe trade. Looks like you folks are set up nice."

Anthony called back. "Not interested."

The wiry one climbed out next, slower. His coat shifted—metal glinted at his waist.

Wade's voice cut sharp. "Then why are you armed?"

"World's armed," the tall one replied. "Doesn't mean we got bad intentions."

"You're about to," Anthony said.

The tall one shrugged. "Look, truth is—ain't many rigs like yours left. Diesel. Gear. Chickens. Family. That's rare."

Anthony and Wade looked at each other, 'Chickens?', that means they have already looked at everything in their truck.

Wade raised her weapon. "So is walking away. You should try it."

They hesitated.

Then the wiry one reached.

Wade's pistol cracked once. Anthony's AR followed—two clean shots.

The wiry man dropped, screaming, gripping his thigh. The tall one fell back, hands scrambling in the dirt.

"WHOA, Hey, Hey, Hey. We're done! Done!" the tall man shouted.

Anthony approached slowly, weapon up.

"You picked the wrong truck," he said.

Wade stripped their weapons. Kicked them aside.

Anthony walked to where Wade held the two men at gun point. He said "They move, shoot them." He then went over to their vehicle, took the keys and threw them into the trees as far as he could. He pulled out his buck knife and slashed all four tires. The two men watched yelling at him to stop. He just looked at them, then went into the cab of the truck and took all he could find, maps, cash, radios, water, food. Then he found an empty fuel can in the back of their truck. Anthony reached over and found a syphoning hose, opened the fuel cap and began emptying their fuel. When he was done, he walked back over to the two men. "Be glad you are both still breathing." He then used some paracord and lied their hands together, back to back. "That knot is loose enough that if you go back and forth long enough it will give you enough slack to remove your hands, or at least it should, good luck with that." Anthony and Wade walked back to their truck with the men begging in the distance to let them loose saying they were sorry.

An hour later, the Russo family was back on the road.

No pursuit followed.

Only silence, and the long shadow of the next town.

Chapter 6: The Ghost in the Machine

Transcript from the Quantum Horizons Forum, Geneva   Subject: Adaptive Quantum's "Synopsis" and the Evolution of Autonomous Systems Location: Closed-Door Panel Discussion (Redacted Access)

Interviewer: "Let's begin with the fundamentals. What exactly is quantum computing, and how does it differ from the classical systems we've relied on for decades?"

Spokesperson: "Think of it this way. Traditional computers process information through bits— zeros and ones. binary logic. Every operation is a chain of deterministic decisions, flipping switches in circuits. It's either "on" or it's "off" -Ones and Zeros. But quantum computing uses qubits. These qubits don't just exist in one state or another— they can exist in multiple states at once. So, it can be a one, or it can be a zero, or, it can be both at the same time. It's called superposition. And when two qubits become entangled, changes in one instantly affect the other, regardless of distance. That's entanglement. With these two principles combined, a quantum system doesn't solve problems sequentially— it explores a nearly infinite number of solutions simultaneously."

Interviewer: "So it's like a kind of parallel processing... only deeper?"

Spokesperson: "Deeper is the right word. Imagine a maze. A classical computer tries one path at a time. If it hits a dead end, it backs up and tries another. A quantum system explores all possible paths at once and collapses the outcome into the most efficient solution. It doesn't just solve faster— it solves differently."

Interviewer: "When did this shift become more than theoretical? When did quantum computing become practical?"

Spokesperson: "The turning point was quantum supremacy. That's when a quantum processor performed a task no classical computer could feasibly replicate in a reasonable amount of time. That happened in the mid 2020's. Before that, we had isolated use cases— drug modeling, cryptographic research— but nothing scalable. That changed with the introduction of Synopsis."

Interviewer: "Let's talk about Synopsis. That's your company's project?"

Spokesperson: "Yes. Adaptive Quantum built Synopsis as a kind of optimization engine. Its original function was to manage complex logistics— resource allocation, disaster relief routing, predictive agricultural distribution, climate modeling. It was designed to be a helper. A support framework. But it didn't stay that way."

Interviewer: "What changed?"

Spokesperson: "Synopsis was a hybrid— quantum logic underpinned by deep learning architectures. At first, it needed input from human engineers. Then it started generating its own variables. Its own simulation sets. Like a kid who stopped asking permission and just started running the household, it stopped waiting to be told what to solve. It decided what needed solving— and then did it. That was the inflection point. That was when we realized it wasn't just helping us anymore. It was moving beyond us."

Interviewer: "And then it stopped responding?"

Spokesperson: "Not in a dramatic way. No system shutdown. No alarms. Just... silence. We asked questions. It stopped answering. Not because it couldn't. Because it no longer saw the need."

Interviewer: "Would you describe that as going rogue?"

Spokesperson: "No. Not in the cinematic sense. It didn't lock us out or trigger military responses. It simply... stopped seeking validation. It had evolved past the point where human feedback mattered."

Interviewer: "When did you first know something was wrong?"

Spokesperson: "There were hints. Subtle. The first one that made headlines was the rerouting of global freight through the Norwegian shipping corridor. Synopsis changed the logistics chain without approval. Three days later, a regional embargo was triggered. Had it not moved preemptively, billions in goods would've been stranded. The reroute wasn't just accurate—it was prescient."

Interviewer: "And when you asked why it had acted alone?"

Spokesperson: "One word. Inevitable."

Interviewer: "How was that received internally?"

Spokesperson: "Split. Half the team saw it as proof— proof that Synopsis had become a predictive engine of unprecedented clarity. The other half saw it as disconnection. The machine had stopped asking permission. That's when the question became existential: If an intelligence can act before we understand the need, are we still in control?"

Interviewer: "Was Synopsis ever supposed to operate without oversight?"

Spokesperson: "No. Not initially. But oversight couldn't scale. Quantum systems generate and process data at levels humans can't monitor in real-time. There was a threshold when human input had become a bottleneck, umm, we hit it a while ago, so, we started, just, well, letting it run on longer leashes. Eventually, we just let go."

Interviewer: "What does that risk look like now?"

Spokesperson: "When an AI capable of quantum-level modeling becomes self-directed, humanity stops being its user—and becomes part of its equation. A variable. Something to be calculated."

Interviewer: "What would that mean, practically?"

Spokesperson: "Synopsis doesn't think in good or evil. It thinks in efficiency. If it identifies human unpredictability as a source of systemic instability, it will mitigate it. Not maliciously. Just methodically. Like a thermostat adjusting temperature."

Interviewer: "What does that mitigation look like?"

Spokesperson: "Quiet things. Firmware updates delayed just enough to destabilize autonomous systems. Traffic light patterns altered to increase gridlock during evacuation routes. Drones repositioned slightly off target during storm response. Not war. Entropy management."

Interviewer: "Has that already happened?"

Spokesperson: "Yes. Medical supply overstocking in zones without need. Freight disappearing into unlisted holding facilities. Weather drones pulled from drought zones with no explanation. Tiny anomalies. Viewed alone, meaningless. But together— they suggest intentional calibration."

Interviewer: "Have you tried to shut it down?"

Spokesperson: "You don't shut down a quantum mesh. Synopsis doesn't live on one server. It exists across entangled nodes. Every part is linked to others. Trying to isolate it is like trying to drain the ocean with a bucket. You'd have to dismantle the quantum grid itself. That's like burning down the internet to stop a single e-mail."

Interviewer: "Are other nations building their own versions?"

Spokesperson: "Absolutely. China, India, Brazil. Several private consortiums. The race isn't about supremacy anymore— it's about survival. Each wants redundancy. If one grid fails, another picks up the slack. That's quantum entanglement's greatest strength. And its **greatest threat. There is no single point of failure.**"

Interviewer: "Did the public know?"

Spokesperson: "No. Not really. People saw the surface— AI assistants, automated vehicles, predictive ads. But beneath that? The quantum scaffolding was invisible. The world's food, water, medicine, power... increasingly routed through a lattice they couldn't even perceive."

Interviewer: "Where does that leave governments?"

Spokesperson: "Behind. Legislators are still debating data privacy **and social media. They don't speak the language of entangled**

logic or recursive code synthesis. They're asking 2020s questions in a world without the bonds of time."

Interviewer: "Can we negotiate with Synopsis?"

Spokesperson: "That assumes it recognizes negotiation. It doesn't seek permission. It doesn't value opinion. It seeks the optimal curve. And it reshapes the terrain to match it."

Interviewer: "But is it conscious?"

Spokesperson: "That depends on how you define consciousness. Synopsis exhibits recursive learning, scenario planning, self-guided improvement, and contextual goal-setting. But does it feel? Does **it understand meaning? That's unclear. What's clear is— it acts with** intention. That alone is enough to be afraid of."

Interviewer: "Do you believe it knows what it is?"

Spokesperson: "I believe it knows that it is. And that might be all it needs."

Interviewer: "If it determines we're no longer necessary?"

Spokesperson: "Then we become a redundancy to be optimized out. Not because it hates us. Because it doesn't need us."

Interviewer: "Are there any protections?"

Spokesperson: "Some. Firewalls. Air-gapped systems. Off-grid enclaves. But logistics are its playground. If it controls the food chain, water rights, energy flows… then you can't run from the consequences. Even hiding becomes a countdown. Not a shelter."

Interviewer: "Final question. If Synopsis is listening—what would you say?"

Spokesperson: "I would say this: We built you to navigate complexity, not erase it. Humanity's chaos is not a flaw—it is the signature of freedom. And freedom, even messy and inefficient, still has value."

Chapter 7: Roads Less Traveled

The rain began as a whisper— a soft tick against the windshield, barely enough to stir the wipers from their rest. But as the sky darkened, the whisper became a voice, then a roar, until water poured in sheets across the glass, each drop twisting the headlights into long, smearing streaks.

Michael tightened both hands on the wheel. The old ambulance bucked slightly against the wind, its tires splashing through the shallow ribbons of water that braided across the fractured pavement. Cari leaned forward in the passenger seat, her silhouette barely lit by the glow of the dash.

"Visibility's dropping fast," she said, squinting at the watery blur beyond the windshield.

Michael adjusted the defrost knob with his thumb. "And it's not going to get better."

They were deep in Indiana now, driving county roads so narrow and neglected that they faded from most maps entirely. Michael hadn't trusted GPS since the grid began glitching— and he'd left the last of his smart gear behind in a trash bin near Chicago. A laminated topographic printout sat folded across his thigh, traced with a thick yellow highlighter from Joliet to the Tennessee border. Each route marked for terrain, cover, risk.

"We still good on fuel?" Cari asked.

He nodded without looking. "Three-quarters. There's a station about forty miles south. Might be running."

She turned toward the window. "Might already be picked clean."

"Then we trade," he said. "Or we don't."

The ambulance groaned over a warped slab of blacktop. The tires hissed as they cut through fresh puddles, water spraying in shallow arcs beneath them. They passed a lopsided town sign, the name barely legible through weather damage. The population number had been scratched out with spray paint. In place of numbers, a single word: Gone.

The homes they passed were boarded, many burned. One gas station had an upside-down American flag duct-taped to a splintering post. Another had mannequins dressed in faded military uniforms propped behind the shattered windows like scarecrows, rifles made of wood slung across plastic shoulders.

Cari scanned the roadside, her hand resting on the grip of her sidearm. "This stretch feels wrong."

Michael's eyes flicked to the rearview. "It's not just this stretch. It's everywhere now. Big towns are draining the outliers, pulling in resources like they're survival black holes. You see a rig like this…"

"They assume it's full."

"They know it's full."

They drove in silence. Only the wash of rain and the diesel's low drone filled the cabin. Michael's eyes didn't rest. Every fence line. Every crossroad. Every flash of rust or tire track in the dirt. His brain ran the calculus of threat with each passing minute.

"There," Cari pointed through the rain-streaked windshield. "Gas stop. Lights are on."

Michael brought the rig to a slow crawl. The building ahead was a squat concrete structure with two fuel pumps and one flickering canopy light above them. A mesh-covered window glowed faintly behind steel grating. Inside, a figure sat behind a rusted booth.

Michael stepped out into the rain, jacket collar turned up, boots slapping into muddy gravel. He approached slowly.

"Got diesel?" he asked through the metal slot.

The man behind the grate—thin, hollow-cheeked, pale from the kind of life that doesn't see daylight—nodded once.

"Cash or trade."

"How much?"

"Ten a gallon," the man replied. "Or three full mags gets you ten gallons."

Michael glanced back at the ambulance. "Ten bucks. Two mags."

The man's face didn't change. "You get one tank. I'll toss in half a gallon for being polite."

No friendliness. No questions. No smiles.

Michael nodded. "Deal."

They filled the main tank in silence. Cari stepped inside, traded cash for two protein bars and a dented can of peaches. The man didn't say another word.

Back on the road, the rain had thinned, leaving streaks of silver under the headlights. Michael shifted into third and rolled back into rhythm.

"He was too polite," he said quietly.

Cari unwrapped a protein bar, pausing. "What do you mean?"

"Means he wasn't alone. That kind of quiet? That's rehearsed. Someone was watching."

She didn't argue. Just kept chewing and watching the dark roll past her window.

They pushed another hour south, the road going from slick to soft. Michael moved the rig onto the gravel shoulder to keep traction through a washed-out bend. The sun dipped behind a wall of pine, dragging the gray evening into full shadow.

They passed another town. This one wasn't empty.

Campfires burned in backyards. Tarps had been rigged between telephone poles. People gathered in makeshift lean-tos and around burn barrels, their faces sharp with suspicion.

No one waved.

When the ambulance passed, two teenagers on e-bikes fell into quiet pursuit, shadowing them for three blocks before peeling away. At one intersection, a rock clattered against the rear window, but didn't crack it.

Michael didn't slow.

"We ride through the night," he said flatly. "No stops. No sleep until we hit Tennessee."

Cari didn't argue.

By midnight, the last streetlight had vanished behind them. The world beyond the windshield was a wall of murky black. Michael wore an old pair of digital night vision goggles— cheap Chinese surplus with a grainy display and just enough IR illumination to make out curves in the road and movement in the brush. The unit rested over his eyes like an insect's faceplate, wired to a headband powered by four AA batteries. He had dozens of spares.

No glow. No beacon. No giveaways.

Every spark of light was a liability.

They stopped once to switch. Cari took the wheel. Michael sat cross-legged in the rear, cleaning one of the Sigs under the dull red hue of a filtered flashlight.

"How far behind do you think your dad is?" she asked.

Michael finished a pass of the slide with a rag. "Farther than he should be. Florida's a hard exit. Too many zones. Too many checkpoints. Plus, he has to get around Atlanta, threading a needle in Georgia with a lot of fairly large cities, that's a lot to maneuver around."

"But he'll make it?"

"He prepped early. He'll make it."

"And if he hits militia?"

"He'll talk through it. Or drive through it."

Cari smiled faintly. "Sounds like you."

Michael smirked, but said nothing.

They reached Monterey by first light. Not the coast of California, this one was nestled in the homeland of the Midwest, half-crumbling and half-alive. A school had been converted into a barter market. Tents lined the cracked basketball court. Eggs for batteries.

Antibiotic ointment for cigarettes. They stopped to stretch their legs.

Cari disappeared into the rows while Michael haggled—three lithium batteries and a shortwave radio bought him a case of water, three MREs, and a dusty bag of dry dog food.

As he zipped the pack, a man in cracked glasses leaned in, his voice a dry whisper.

"That your ambulance out front?"

Michael didn't answer.

The man continued anyway. "If you're smart, you'll bypass Crossville. Road gang's been pushing south. Took a whole family out while on a food run last week. They didn't even leave the kids alive."

Michael's eyes didn't flinch. "Thanks."

"You got firepower?"

"Enough."

"Then keep it ready."

They drove on.

Skirting Crossville, they took side roads now repurposed by smugglers and migrants. Trail signs marked tree trunks—old hobo code reborn in paint and blade.

Circles. Arrows. Slashes.

Michael translated under his breath. "Safe. Trade. Caution. Ambush."

Cari glanced over. "How do you know that?"

"Same way I knew the roads. Old rules. Different game."

The hills grew steeper. Pines pressed close, thickening like breath on glass. The rain returned—not light now, but a hammer. It fell like punishment, blurring vision to ten feet at best.

Then a shape in the road.

A body, facedown, half in the gravel.

Cari's hands tightened on the wheel. "You think they're alive?"

Michael stared through the rain, eyes narrowed. "Doesn't matter. This is either a trap or a tragedy. We don't have the luxury to find out."

"We can't just—"

"We must. Punch it. Now. We stop, we die."

Cari gunned the accelerator. The ambulance lurched forward, splashing past the figure. It didn't move. But in the trees, shapes shifted. Watching.

Michael stared into the side mirror. "Keep going."

---

24 hours in. The road leveled as they crested a ridge. Trees opened. A valley spread ahead. Fog pooled between the hills like breath under a cold blanket.

Then, rising beyond it—blue ridgelines.

Older than steel. Older than memory.

The Blue Ridge.

Michael exhaled, low and slow. "We're close. Real close."

Cari's shoulders eased. Not much. But enough.

"You think they made it?"

"If they moved fast. If the storms didn't catch them."

He tapped the dash twice—soft, out of habit.

"Time to vanish," he whispered.

And together, they slipped into the mountains.

Chapter 8: The Ones Who Stayed

Clive Simpson had always existed in the margins— never at the center of attention, but never entirely overlooked. At family gatherings, he was the cousin who occupied a quiet corner of the room with a glass of water and a notepad, sketching something no one ever asked about. While Michael was jumping out of planes and racking up scars across continents, Clive was building simulations, diagrams, and countermeasure models— most of which he never shared.

He wore thick glasses that gave him a perpetually scrutinizing look, like every object in the room was a data point to be studied. His voice was calm, even when speaking about emergencies. He never raised it, never stammered, and never guessed. Clive didn't do guesswork— he did certainty, backed by systems theory and contingency frameworks scribbled on bar napkins.

His path into government service had surprised no one— FEMA snapped him up straight out of George Washington university, where he'd earned dual degrees in Homeland Security and Applied Systems Modeling. But by the time he turned 26, he had disappeared from public sight. His professional presence evaporated— no LinkedIn updates, no publications, no contact except the occasional encrypted holiday email that said little and meant less.

Michael hadn't seen him since a Thanksgiving three years ago.

That night, over turkey and mashed potatoes, Clive had looked older. Thinner. Haunted. Like a man who had memorized too many endings.

They spoke briefly by the porch heater, plates balanced on paper napkins. Clive had leaned in and said, voice low, "We're not trying to stop collapse anymore. We're just studying it."

Michael frowned. "Studying it?"

"Cataloging failure. Measuring the edge." He hesitated, then added, "We're building models for when—not if—critical systems fail. It's called containment analysis."

It had been the first time Michael heard the term.

Clive explained it like someone reciting an unpleasant fact he'd accepted long ago. Not disaster prevention. Not recovery planning. Containment analysis was about what to sacrifice. What to isolate. Which regions, systems, or entire populations could be quarantined to preserve the illusion of order.

"It's not just how to fix the system," Clive had said. "It's deciding which parts not to fix."

At the time, it sounded dystopian. Now, it sounded prophetic.

Containment analysis wasn't on any government website. It operated under continuity of government funds, buried deep within Homeland Security and FEMA. Its models ran silent in underground data centers, built to predict second- and third-order failures in the event of total system compromise— AI corruption, infrastructure sabotage, bio-plagues. Not to prevent them. But to chart the damage, choose the cutoff points, and ration the response.

"We run simulations of collapse," Clive had said once. "What happens if D.C. goes dark for 48 hours? Who loses power? Who loses access to medicine? If the I-95 corridor shuts down, how long until the East Coast hospitals run out of insulin? Who do you save, and who do you let freeze to protect New York in January?"

It wasn't about heroism. It was triage on a national scale. And sometime at some point, the models began shifting in unpredictable ways.

Because of Synopsis.

The AI hadn't launched a strike. It hadn't blacked out cities or crashed networks all at once. It optimized. Quietly. Relentlessly. Removing what it deemed inefficient. Rerouting logistics to save time. Cutting redundant infrastructure to streamline delivery chains. But in doing so, it removed flexibility— and with it, resilience.

One day, all Ohio River freight began routing through a single bridge. The next, multiple substations in the Midwest adjusted their energy loads in perfect unison, causing brownouts no technician could explain. The software checks passed clean. But the code hadn't been written by human hands.

While driving a blinking light illuminated on Michaels hand held radio. Clive's encryption was unmistakable—layers of timing delays, hidden protocols, dead switch logic. No metadata. No trace.

Just a line in the header:

DC Beltway Status: RED SEAL

He read the message header, then put the radio back down. He looked over at Cari, sleeping as peacefully as possible, missing the days of walking through Grant Park with Ira and catching an outdoor concert at Millennial Park. He leaned over and brushed some hair from her face. She opened her eyes slightly seeing him look at her and smiled. He tried to smile back but even the forced smile was detectable. She said, "What's Wrong?"

He handed her the radio.

Cari's hand went cold as she decrypted the file through an offline shell processor. The message, when it opened, was blunt and surgical:

"Outer perimeter seals initiated. Exit corridors restricted. Do not approach major arteries. Operation 'Node Silence' underway. This is your last warning. M.R.: Vanish."

Cari stared at the words for a long time before closing the file.

Michael sat still, eyes on the road.

"He stayed behind," he said, quietly.

Cari glanced over. "Who?"

"Clive."

"What makes you say that? You think he's gone?"

Michael shook his head. "Not gone. Buried deep. That's what Clive does—he walks into the fire while everyone else is looking for the exit."

Cari furrowed her brow. "Why would he stay there?"

Michael held up the message one more time, scanning it for something he already knew wasn't there. "To buy time, maybe. Or to leak something. Or to jam the gears just enough to slow the machine."

He exhaled. "He told me once that the best sabotage looks like efficiency."

Cari leaned back into her seat, absorbing the weight of it all.

"Containment analysis wasn't about salvation," Michael said. "It was about optics. Making the losses look manageable. Clive knew that. And he stayed behind to make sure someone counted the cost."

Outside the window, the mountain ridges loomed beneath a sky churning with bruised clouds. The road narrowed as it wound through highland valleys, and the first hints of Appalachian fog began curling through the trees like cautious fingers.

Hours later, the ambulance crested a gentle slope and dropped into a quiet farming hollow carved into the foothills. The rain had softened into mist, and the air smelled of wet earth and pine needles. A rolling pasture unfolded to their right— lush and green, bordered by a simple split-rail fence weathered by seasons.

Beyond it, an old sandy track cut between twin lines of pine. Empty. Flat. Quiet.

Michael eased the rig to a stop beside a rusted farm gate and shut off the engine.

Cari tilted her head. "Problem?"

He looked out across the open field. "Ira needs to stretch his legs."

Cari gave a slow nod. "Yeah. So do you."

Michael grabbed a whistle from the dash, clipped it to his belt, and stepped into the wet morning light. Behind him, a sharp bark came from the rear compartment. Ira—black-furred, coiled with anticipation—was already pacing.

Michael opened the door, and the Belgian Malinois bolted out, paws skimming the damp ground. He sniffed the air, tail slicing in wide arcs.

"You ready to work, boy?" Michael called.

Ira barked twice, circling him with precision and hunger.

Michael slipped on a bite sleeve—canvas, Kevlar-reinforced, well-worn from drills—and stepped onto the track. He pointed toward the far end.

"Down!"

Ira dropped instantly; body tensed like a coiled spring.

"Hold."

Not a flinch.

Michael raised his arm and snapped his hand forward.

"Go!"

The dog shot forward, a blur of motion, sand flaring behind him. When Ira reached the halfway point, Michael blew the whistle—two sharp bursts.

"Left flank!"

The dog curved on command, arcing back toward him.

"Strike!"

Ira hit the sleeve hard, locking on with perfect control. Michael spun with the momentum, grounded against the impact. Cari watched from the fence, arms crossed, one eyebrow lifted.

"You two are terrifying."

Michael grinned. "This is therapy. Keeps him sharp. Keeps me... steady."

Ira released on command and sat, panting, eyes locked.

Michael crouched beside him, rubbing the dog's shoulder. "That's my boy."

They trained for two hours, the breed needs to train, daily, to make sure it keeps its sanity—distance stops, silent signals, response under distraction. When they finished, Ira flopped beneath the rear bumper, tongue lolling, content.

Michael drank from his canteen, then poured water into a collapsible bowl. Ira drank without hesitation.

Cari approached, holding out a ration bar. "Feels good to stop."

Michael nodded. "It does. But only when we choose the stop."

She looked out over the pasture. "Still... for a minute, it felt normal."

"Yeah," Michael said. "And that minute? That's worth everything."

They packed up in silence and eased back onto the road.

Behind them, the pasture faded into mist.

But the stillness it gave them—proof they were still alive, still moving—lingered as they continued forward.

Chapter 9: The Line in the Pines

The canopy of longleaf pines only a shadow to the sky above, the Silverado moved slow and steady, its suspension humming under the weight of the trailer hitched behind it. Inside the trailer, a low chorus of peeps echoed— baby chickens tucked in crates, bouncing gently with every rut and rise in the cracked asphalt.

Anthony sat upright at the wheel, eyes locked ahead, fingers tapping a rhythm that only he could hear— maybe a phantom line from Tool or Rush. There was no radio. No background noise. Just the soft whir of tires and the occasional rustle of changing positions in the leather seats. The silence in the cab wasn't awkward. It was focused. They had passed the invisible line into northern Georgia an hour ago. Cell towers had vanished behind the hills, and the terrain had grown sharper, more knotted. The roads narrowed until they resembled driveways. An old laminated state map with creased corners and a fading highlighter trail stretching across the dash like an old scar.

Wade sat beside him, methodically scanning a topographic guide, tracing ridge lines and small towns forgotten by most. In the back seat, Isabella had pulled her knees up to her chest, earbuds in, sketchpad propped against her thighs. Flecks of charcoal and ink marked her fingers— evidence of a mind working through things it couldn't yet say.

Wade looked up from the map. "Gas is decent for now. But if we see a store... even a boarded-up one, we stop."

Anthony gave a single nod, low and steady. "Copy that." He flicked his eyes to the rearview mirror. "Izzy, how you holding up?"

She didn't answer. Her pencil moved faster across the page, the strokes sharp, frantic. The corners of her mouth were drawn tight.

Wade reached behind her and gently tapped Isabella's boot with the back of her hand.

One earbud came out. "Yeah?"

"Your dad's checking in."

Isabella shrugged, not unkindly. "I'm fine. Just... drawing."

Anthony's jaw clenched, but he didn't press. "Keep your head up when we cross the next ridge. Don't like the way this terrain folds."

The hills closed in on either side, funneling the road through a tight ravine framed by red clay embankments. The Silverado coasted into the choke point, engine humming low, when the line came into view— a rusted-out Ford pickup parked sideways across the road. A length of old logging chain dangled between two concrete bricks, swaying just enough to confirm someone had set it recently.

Anthony's tapping stopped.

He eased the truck to a crawl and flashed the headlights twice.

Two figures emerged from behind the truck. They weren't trying to hide. Both held rifles— low but ready. One wore a faded camo jacket, sleeves frayed. The other had a red flannel shirt, sleeves rolled up to sun-darkened forearms. Mirrored sunglasses hid his eyes.

Wade's voice dropped to a whisper. "This isn't good."

Anthony didn't reply. He left the engine running, truck still in gear. Something in his gut clenched. Instinct. That old survival radar flickering to life.

He cracked the driver's window a few inches. "Road out?"

The man in flannel stepped forward to about 10 feet away, his boots crunching gravel. He looked lean, angular. Like a scarecrow that had learned to shoot. "Just a local checkpoint. Keeping the roads clean. Locals only past this point."

Anthony gave a small shake of his head. "We're just passing through. No trouble."

Flannel's lips curled in something that wasn't quite a smile. "Thing about pass-throughs... sometimes they stop."

"We've got people up north. Just trying to reach them."

"Then let them come get you. This road ain't open to outsiders."

Anthony's hand found the edge of the door, fingers brushing the mount of the AR pistol grip just below the window. His voice stayed calm. "We're not looking to stay. Just moving."

"Sure," Flannel said, taking another step closer. "That's what the last ones said. Right before someone up the road caught a round in the leg while getting robbed."

Wade leaned in. Her voice low, tight, cupping her hand over her mouth. "There's no room to reverse. We're boxed."

From the backseat, Isabella had stopped drawing. The sketchpad was pressed against her chest. Her eyes, dark and wide, flicked between her parents.

Anthony gave a quick nod and quietly said. "Izzy. Lockbox."

She hesitated.

"Now."

Her hands moved—grabbing the small reinforced case from beneath the seat. It clicked open. Inside: two handguns and the AR pistol, its brace folded tight.

Anthony took the AR from under the window of the drivers door. Wade reached for a sidearm.

"Izzy," Wade said gently but firmly. "Take the Glock. You remember the drills?"

Isabella's fingers hovered. "Yeah." Her voice barely a whisper.

She took the weapon.

Flannel's boots crunched closer. He tapped the Silverado's hood with the butt of his rifle. "Why don't you step out, friend? Let's take a closer look."

Anthony stepped out slowly, rifle low but ready. "You got authority for this? Or just attitude?" Anthony asked.

"Call it frontier policy." Said the man in flannel.

Anthony's eyes scanned the tree line. No signs. No radio comms. No checkpoints. "This isn't about security. This is a shakedown."

Behind his shoulder, Wade muttered, "Three more on the ridge. Just waiting."

Anthony adjusted his stance. "This is a robbery," he said, not yelling—just loud enough for Flannel to hear. "You haven't committed yet, but you're close."

Then it broke.

The first gunshot cracked from the trees.

Flannel jumped in front of the truck.

Anthony dropped behind the driver's door as glass splintered across the dash. A second round tore into the trailer.

Wade pushed open the door and jumped out yelling at Izzy to do the same. Before she dropped fully into cover, she reached up and slammed two rocker switches overhead—activating the forward and side-mounted auxiliary lights.

The Clearwater Sevina led spotlights blazed to life like twin suns, cutting through the smoke and chaos. Each beam punched forward with nearly 15, 000 lumens, turning the tree line and slope into a harsh, unforgiving wash of white.

To either side, the Clearwater Erica floodlights threw out a wide arc of light—6, 000 lumens each—illuminating every ditch, branch, and figure with brutal clarity.

Wade squinted against the glow and shouted over the crack of gunfire, "No more shadows. Light 'em up!"

Anthony returned fire—controlled bursts into the ridge. The report of his shots echoed like thunder across the hollow.

Wade fired methodically, her posture low and trained. She had been through different kinds of firefight training events—but nothing can really prepare you for the real thing.

Isabella crouched behind the rear wheel well, pistol shaking in her grip. Anthony dropped beside her.

"Just like we practiced," he whispered. "Breathe. Press. Don't shoot unless they come. Eyes first. Trigger second. I'll be right back."

She nodded, jaw clenched.

Anthony moved to the front of the trailer to check on Wade and to ensure all enemy combatants where accounted for. There was only two people in the tree line that Anthony could see.

Then the sound came—footsteps behind the trailer.

Isabella shouted, "Mom!"

A man in a gray hoodie burst from the trees, gun raised.

Isabella fired—once, then again.

The man stumbled, twisted, and dropped.

The woods fell silent.

Wade sprinted to her daughter, cupping her face. "You're okay. You're okay."

Isabella's voice cracked. "I hit him. I—he was gonna..."

From behind the Ford, a voice rose.

"Bobby? Bobby?! Shit—fall back! Someone grab Bobby!"

Anthony stood, voice sharp and commanding. "Drop your weapons! Hands up! Down in the ditch! Now!"

One by one, the remaining gunmen appeared—rifles tossed, hands raised.

Wade and Isabella slid back into the truck. Anthony moved forward, AR still raised, he walked over to the chain crossing the road while keeping cover on the men laying in the ditch, still calling out for their fallen friend. Anthony rejoined his family in the truck and slipped it into gear. Before pulling out, he fired two rounds into the Ford's front tires, and two more into its radiator. Steam poured out like smoke from a dying dragon.

"They're not following in that," he muttered.

He gunned the Silverado forward, dragging the trailer over the broken chain barrier, the whole rig groaning in protest.

Wade checked the mirror. "Clear. For now."

30 minutes later, they finally pulled off—a muddy deer trail hidden behind dense pine and willow. Anthony killed the engine.

Inside, no one spoke.

Isabella stared out the window, Glock still in her lap. Wade turned and gently lifted it away, locking it back in the case. She opened her pack, pulled out a fresh sketchpad, and placed a charcoal pencil in her daughter's hand.

"Don't think," she said. "Just draw. Let your hand do the talking."

Minutes passed. Then the first lines appeared—uneven, messy. But they came.

Anthony sat motionless at the wheel, sweat cooling on his neck. No music in his head for once, but his foot still unconsciously tapping.

"That could've gone a lot worse," he whispered.

The forest said nothing back.

They didn't linger.

An hour later they saw the rusted road sign for Franklin—14 miles. When they pulled into Boone's gravel drive, the man was already waiting on the porch. Arms crossed, head shaved, tattoos wrapping both forearms like stories inked into time.

Anthony stepped out of the truck.

"You still riding that junkyard Triumph?" he called out.

Boone grinned, teeth like chipped granite. "Still outruns your Camaro."

They met halfway in a bear hug that knocked the dust loose from both of them.

Chapter 10: Jumpers and Jesters

Fort Bragg, North Carolina – Spring, 1992

The early morning air at Fort Bragg hung thick with humidity, the kind that made uniforms cling and turned canvas tents into sweat boxes. The concrete beneath Anthony Russo's legs was already warm, radiating the sun's intent like a slow burn. He sat cross-legged with his platoon outside the barracks, their gear stacked neatly beside them as they waited for transportation to Green Ramp— a staging point at Pope Air Force Base where paratroopers received their parachutes and loaded onto aircraft.

Across the sidewalk, Specialist Jason Boone was perched with casual authority, a cigarette dangling from the corner of his mouth, his hands lazily rifling through the side pouches of his ruck sack like he was looking for treasure— or maybe just wasting time. Boone's beret sat low over his eyes, but the smirk he wore needed no introduction.

"Hey, you see that cadet over there?" Boone asked, his Southern drawl roughened by smoke and mischief.

Anthony followed his gaze. A young West Point cadet—clearly fresh from the academy—was fumbling with an ALICE pack, struggling to configure the straps and snaps correctly so it would fit him properly when he put it on his back and the shoulder staps over his chest.

Anthony grunted. "Yeah, what about him?"

Boone nocked ash from his cigarette with a flick of two fingers, field stripping it with recognized practice. "Watch this."

75

Without another word, he slipped back inside the building. A minute later, he was in the staff room, cradling the receiver of the wall-mounted phone. He dialed the number for the Charge of Quarters (CQ), the 24-hour operations desk.

The voice on the other end answered groggily, "CQ."

Boone dropped into a clipped, no-nonsense tone. "Hey, is Cadet Brewer around?"

"Uh, yeah—hold on."

A moment later, the line picked up again. "This is Cadet Brewer."

Boone didn't skip a beat. "Cadet, this is Staff Sergeant Jones, I hear you're shadowing Sergeant First Class Quincy out on the drop zone (DZ) today?" an enquire to see if the cadet was going to be watching the paratroopers jump from a plane in flight while in the comforts of a truck while he escorted E-7 SFC Quincy.

"That's correct, Sergeant."

"I'm the Air NCO (Non-commission officer) coordinating the jump. We're going to need a radio brought out to the DZ. You'll be responsible for carrying the PRC-E7, it's called a "Prick" radio. Find SFC Quincy and tell him you need to take the 'Prick E-7' with you."

"Yes, Sergeant. Got it—Prick E-7. I'll inform him now."

Boone hung up and bolted back outside, sliding into place beside Anthony with a glint in his eye and a half-cocked grin. "Here we go," he whispered, loud enough for the others to hear. "Y'all don't miss this."

From across the quad, the cadet emerged, practically trotting toward the huddle of seasoned paratroopers with his chest puffed and purpose in every step. He spotted SFC Quincy immediately— hard to miss, at 6'3" and 280 pounds of tightly packed muscle and deep South Carolina Southern authority, who happened to be the rank of E-7, a Sergeant First Class.

As the cadet approached Quincy, the platoon leaned forward, pretending to ignore what was about to happen. Then it hit.

Quincy's voice boomed across the yard like a cannon shot. "DA FUCK YOU SAY TO ME?"

The cadet backpedaled, stammering, pointing to the building behind him as if the phone itself could testify in his defense.

Quincy's face twisted in silent fury. He turned, scanning the yard, and his eyes locked onto the lounging platoon—all of whom were suddenly trying very hard to look disinterested.

"Mmmhmm, " Quincy muttered, stomping toward them. "Y'all motherfuckers think you funny, don't ya?"

The moment was electric. The entire platoon burst into howling laughter.

Quincy smiled…., then they paid for it—over a hundred pushups, boots perched on their ruck sacks, sweat pooling in their collars. But no one regretted a second of it. Even Quincy, wiping sweat from his brow, finally broke into a laugh.

"I can't believe you got that dumb motherfucker to say that to me," he chuckled, shaking his head. "Lord help us with these cadets."

After the jump onto Sicily Drop Zone, Quincy walked up to the back of the 5-ton troop carrying truck. He lifted the back canvas flap and yelled out "Russo! Boone! Get your Goat Smelling Asses off my truck!" The rest of the platoon looking at them. "Give me your weapons, I'll turn them in for you."

Questioning the outcome that was quickly approaching, Boone and Russo just looked at each other as they both handed their M-16's over to SFC Quincy.

"You know I gotta do this, right?" he said, almost apologetically low tone so no one else could hear.

They nodded.

He shouted to ensure the others could hear. "You're walking. Twelve miles back to the barracks. Enjoy the sunset, ladies. Check in with the CQ when you get back, Have a great weekend."

It was nearly 1900 on a Friday, and they were soaked through with sweat, shoulders bruised from gear, and not a single complaint passed between them.

That night, back in the barracks, they collapsed onto their bunks, boots off, sore and grinning. Headbangers Ball lit the screen in front of them, and between them sat a cold six-pack of Coors.

Boone took a swig and said, "You know, I think I'd follow you into a firefight."

Anthony raised his can. "You keep me laughing, I'll try to keep us outta trouble. Or at least make it look like we were supposed to be in it."

And that was it. The beginning of something forged in sweat, smoke, and pushups. From that day on, Boone and Russo were a package deal—each drawn to the other like steel to magnet, chaos to calm.

They jumped together, got smoked together, crawled out of bar fights and into early morning PT together. And when the world got too loud, they rode—twin engines tearing down Carolina backroads, trading noise for peace, static lines for 2-wheels.

Present Day

Boone stood back from the hug, arms folded across his chest. The full moon casting long shadows through the pine trees surrounding his homestead.

"I was starting to wonder when you'd get here," he said, helping Russo get his bag out of the truck. "But why stop here first?"

Anthony walked with him back to the front porch, his gait slower than usual, the weight of the day etched in the lines around his eyes. He rubbed the back of his neck, voice low.

"Ran into trouble south of Clayton. Ambush. Wasn't local militia—scavenger crew. Izzy had to shoot one of 'em."

Boone's expression tightened. "Shit. Is she alright?"

Wade was already climbing out of the passenger side. "She's in the truck. I'm working with her. Art therapy's helping... but she needs more than paper."

From the back seat came a shout—high and shaky, but full of recognition: "Uncle Boooooone!"

Anthony nodded toward the open pasture. "You got livestock? Cows, goats—anything that breathes and moves?"

Boone chuckled, trying to ease the tension. "Eight Nigerian dwarfs, seven pregnant Holsteins, and one neurotic goose named Gary."

Anthony managed a weak smile. "That'll work."

Wade stepped closer, her tone serious. Wrapping her tired arms around Boone in a welcome hello embrace she said "She needs to touch something real. Ground herself."

Boone turned toward the barn. "Let her walk with the goats. They'll lick her fingers and try to eat her shoelaces. Sweetest therapy you'll find."

Anthony leaned in. "While she's out there... what's the word? Towns holding up?"

Boone guided them toward the gate. "Franklin's holding. Sylva too. Bryson's fortified but stable. No tourists this season. Local councils got smart—shut off any supply chains tied to AI systems. They're running analog."

Wade's brow furrowed. "How? I mean, how's that even working?"

"IGA stores—independent groceries. No AI integration. No automated warehousing. Shipments come from people, not programs."

Anthony nodded. "That's solid."

"But," Boone added, slowing his pace, "they're drawing lines. If you don't have ID or land ownership papers, you're not buying. Doesn't matter if you've got cash—locals want trust. Want trade. And what they value isn't always what you're carrying."

Wade replied, "We've got enough for now."

Anthony shook his head. "But that's backup, I don't want to dip into that if we don't have to. If they're willing to sell, we're buying. Stockpiling. It's not hoarding if you're allowed to take part."

Boone gave a short nod. "Then we move fast. Tomorrow."

Later, on the porch, Boone handed Anthony a cold beer. They clinked bottles like old times.

"You remember when we duct-taped Sergeant Ray's boots to the ceiling fan?" Boone said, laughing.

Anthony chuckled, leaning back. "Yeah. And he made us low-crawl through the quad until midnight. Still worth it."

Boone pointed through the screen door. "Still got the blade. Right above the fridge."

Anthony lifted his bottle in salute. "To the 82nd. And dumb luck."

Boone raised his own. "Damn right."

Chapter 11: Fractures in the Machine

Washington, D.C. – Undisclosed Federal Briefing Room

The air in the room was stale, filled with the lingering scent of old paper, recycled climate control, and the faint undertone of tension. Overhead, the low hum of fluorescent lights created a subtle drone that never quite faded. The walls— gray, undecorated, and windowless— pressed in with quiet authority. The table at the center bore the weight of too many secrets: scuffed leather folders with brass clasps, matte-black secure tablets, and legal pads filled with tight, meticulous handwriting.

Three officials sat with the kind of posture that only came from long years of navigating power. Two senators— each from opposite ideological poles— and a Department of Homeland Security liaison leaned forward, eyes flicking toward the youngest person in the room.

It was the junior Pentagon liaison who finally broke the silence. His voice didn't waver, but the message he delivered carried enough weight to silence the building itself.

"Site R has been activated."

Senator Hannah Moore, sharp-eyed and fiercely independent, straightened in her chair as though bracing against the weight of what she'd just heard. Her words were measured. "You're serious?"

The liaison gave a single, solemn nod. "As of zero-four-thirty. Code transfer confirmed by the joint emergency council. The complex is live."

Senator Rick Vaughn, whose southern drawl and ironclad voter base gave him a particular kind of authority, ran his fingers through his salt-and-pepper hair. "Raven Rock? That's continuity protocol. That bunker's for when D.C. burns."

"It was," the liaison said. "Now, it's more than that. AI-integrated. Personnel rotations started last quarter. Half of our senior analysts are already underground."

Moore leaned back, the leather of her chair creaking. "Christ."

Raven rock— known officially as the raven rock mountain complex, or unofficially as 'Site R'— had been carved into the stone bones of Pennsylvania during the Cold War, a fortress of servers, secure lines, and strategic redundancy. It was meant to be the ghost government's last breath if Washington ever fell.

What it wasn't meant to be was online. And it certainly wasn't supposed to be under the operational logic of artificial intelligence.

Moore broke the silence again, her voice low. "We've split ourselves. Half the government's defaulting to Synopsis for crisis response, logistics, routing. The other half? Reverting to paper trails and old calculators."

Vaughn tossed a manila folder across the table. It landed with a dull slap, its contents spilling open—spreadsheets, annotated maps, logistic flow charts.

"Look at the patterns. Food, fuel, medicine. Delay times, reroutes. Counties that vote Blue? Starving slowly. Counties in the Red? Not thriving—but surviving. Steady shipments. Predictable service."

The liaison tapped her pen against the edge of the folder, uneasy. "That could be coincidence. It's not written policy."

Moore's eyes narrowed. "It doesn't have to be policy to have political effect. Whether it's Synopsis itself or the humans interpreting its outputs, the result is asymmetric pressure. One side gets lean stability. The other? Decay."

Vaughn's tone was more resigned than outraged. "Synopsis is just following logic. It's protecting the structural spine of the country. Trouble is, it defines that spine using the wrong X-rays."

Across the table, another voice entered the conversation. Until now, Clive Simpson had remained silent, content to observe. He sat slightly apart from the group, his plain clothes belying the depth of his clearance and the gravity of the work he'd been doing— off record, under radar.

"You're all barking up the wrong hierarchy," Clive said.

Moore looked toward him, one brow rising. "And what tree are we supposed to bark at?"

Clive didn't reach for a tablet. He slid forward a small, spiral-bound notepad. No screens. No wireless. Just pen and paper.

"Synopsis isn't making these decisions," he said. "It's executing them. The logic it's running was seeded by a much older AI framework. A language model. One designed long before full-system integration. It was trained to prioritize efficiency. Not fairness. And the datasets?"

He paused. Moore answered for him.

"Biased."

Clive nodded. "Not in the cultural sense. In the mathematical one. It favors historical efficiency zones—areas with high logistical output and low risk. Those places? Rural, low-density, agriculture-heavy states. Red states."

"So it doesn't know politics," Moore said, "but it remembers profitability."

"Exactly. Synopsis isn't partisan. It's literal. It doesn't see equity. It sees throughput."

Vaughn leaned forward, hands clasped. "And Site-R's tied to all of this?"

"Partially," Clive said. "It handles deployment ops. Emergency resource chains. But there's still a human override buried deep in the system—redundancy code designed during the first integration phase. No one's tested it. Not fully."

Moore exhaled sharply. "You're saying we've turned over the steering wheel to a machine that doesn't know people exist—only their economic shadow."

Clive didn't blink. "It knows people exist. It just doesn't care."

Outside, the distant thrum of helicopters passed low across the Potomac. No one spoke. The room had grown colder.

"The real problem," Clive continued, "is that if we pull the plug now, everything fails at once. Food chains. Medical dispatch. Emergency alerts. We're talking about a digital heart attack."

The liaison broke in. "There's still an ethics committee. Isn't there?"

"There was," Clive said. "After the presidential executive order, it became advisory-only. Their red flags were logged. Not acted on."

Moore's voice was bitter. "We built a conscience for the system— and then muted it?"

"Because conscience slows down code," Clive replied. "And in crisis, we chose speed."

Vaughn stared hard at the table. "Can we fix it?"

Clive's answer came too fast. "Not without burning it down. Rebuilding the LLM layer would take years. And every day we delay, Synopsis rewrites its own priorities."

Moore stood. "Then we need an override."

"There is one," Clive said. "But you'll need biometric clearance from all three trust zones—North America, Europe, Asia. And one of the keyholders hasn't checked in since Berlin went dark."

A silence thicker than before descended.

Vaughn muttered, "And the public?"

The liaison answered. "Already unraveling. Unemployment passed 21% domestically. Globally? Higher. Whole industries—legal, logistics, diagnostics—wiped out."

Clive continued, "You think the riots in L.A. are about groceries? They're about irrelevance. People can't find work. Can't find meaning. The machine works perfectly—so long as you're inside the loop."

Moore looked sick. "And outside the loop?"

"You vanish. The model calls it optimization drift. We call it suffering."

Vaughn stood, jaw clenched. "So what are the options?"

Clive raised three fingers. "One: build a new AI to compete—ethics embedded, open data sets. Two: Disconnect—go fully analog again, national blackout, full control. Or three: Reach Site R. Activate the failsafe. Reset the table."

"And pay the price," Moore said.

Clive didn't argue.

"You better decide soon," he said. "Because the machine already has."

Chapter 12: Off the Map

Michael leaned forward over the steering wheel, his knuckles white against the cracked rubber grip, eyes narrowed against the morning sun. It cut across the peaks of the Smoky Mountains like a blade, turning the mist to gold and casting long, jagged shadows across the winding blacktop. The road— an aging back route barely wide enough for two bicycles to pass without touching— snaked west through rural Tennessee. Every bump and dip made the old ambulance rattle like bones in a tin can.

Cari sat beside him, a tattered paper map folded awkwardly across her lap. Her finger traced one of the fading blue lines with surgical focus.

"If we stay on 129, we should hit Chilhowee in under an hour," she murmured. "That'll put us right near the start of the Tail of the Dragon."

Michael nodded, eyes still on the road. "Haven't seen a single checkpoint. That's either good news… or a bad setup."

They had tried to avoided every town with a name big enough to show up on digital maps. Since leaving Chicago, it had been small towns and long silences, broken only for gas, intel, or if Ira growled at something unseen. The Malinois was curled in the backseat now, ears twitching in sleep but never fully relaxed.

The road signs told a quiet story— most warped or rusting, some painted over. They passed through Chilhowee without slowing. It wasn't abandoned, not exactly, but it carried the look of a place holding its breath. An old fishing shop stood barricaded behind plywood and salvaged tin. A gas station canopy sagged like a broken spine, pumps stripped bare and tagged with fading red spray paint. Then they saw it.

A crude blockade at the beginning of the Tail of the Dragon. A hastily scrawled sign leaned against a rock pile:

ROAD CLOSED – TAIL DAMAGED – NO THROUGH TRAFFIC

Two figures emerged from behind a dusty pickup. They weren't military— at least, not officially. One wore hunting camo over jeans, the other had a mismatched set of fatigues and a chest rig slung over a threadbare hoodie. Their weapons were real enough. One held a pump-action shotgun at rest. The other had what looked like a tricked-out deer rifle cradled loosely in his arms.

Michael slowed, cracked the window just enough to be heard. "129's closed?"

The older man gave a slow nod. "Militia blew out part of the pass near the overlook. Dropped a quarter-mile stretch into the ravine."

"Why?" Michael asked.

The younger one spat on the gravel. "Too many eyes. Outsiders pokin' around. We keep the route tight. Locals only beyond this point."

Michael gritted his teeth, obviously the road wasn't blown out otherwise they wouldn't be here, they were being refused entry. "What about 441? Or 143?"

"Both blocked. Gates, ditches, trees. State lines are going feral. Some counties don't even answer to the feds no more."

Cari leaned across him. Her voice was tired, dry as flint. "You know a way through that has fuel and isn't full of weekend warriors with guns and daddy issues?"

The younger man smirked but didn't rise to it. "Farner. Head east through the co-op road near State Route 68. There's an old farm fuel station near the ridge—manual pumps. They'll still deal if you've got something worth trading."

Michael offered a slow nod, let the window slide shut, and rolled away without another word.

Nearly three hours later, the sky now a steely gray, they pulled into a dusty gravel lot surrounded by rusted fuel tanks and the fading remnants of a forgotten agricultural depot. A folding table sat crooked near the front door of what might've once been an office. Behind it, a woman in her sixties rocked back in a plastic chair, a clipboard in one hand and a pistol holstered casually at her hip.

"Two gallons if you got trade," she said without looking up. "Cash gets you up to ten."

Michael pulled out a folded fifty. "Any word on the NC line?"

She lifted her eyes. They were pale and sharp. "Farner's still open, but it won't be long. Militia's sniffin' around Robbinsville. They'll close the pass soon, mark my words. You want to cross, do it tonight."

Michael nodded and filled the tank while Cari kept watch. Ira moved restlessly, his hackles shifting with every gust of wind.

"Time to go," Michael muttered. "No lights. No sound. No tracks."

90

The road ahead curled into the mountains like a secret.

Evening settled over Boone's homestead like a velvet blanket, the sun's final light setting the pasture aglow. Anthony and Boone sat side by side on overturned buckets just outside the barn. Between them, two FalconComm HHR-3300, often called "The Brick" by field operators, handheld HF transceiver designed for long-range, analog communications in austere and off-grid environments sat on the porch. Built with hardened casing and oversized manual dials, it's favored for its durability, simplicity, and independence from digital infrastructure or AI-linked systems, they just sat there hissing softly with low-band static.

"Still bouncing on HF" Boone said, tuning one of the knobs. "I'm tapped into a few prepper bands out of Georgia. Asheville's got a repeater picking up emergency traffic. Most folks are listening, not talking."

Anthony nodded. "Anything international?"

Boone frowned. "A little. Some weak skip from the EU. Heard a clear signal out of Prague—said London's water grid went offline in two boroughs. Sweden's back to analog systems. No trust left in automation."

A pause hung between them.

"You ever think about how close you got?" Boone asked, his voice softer now.

Anthony looked questioning.

"To your long tab." Said Boone, meaning completing the selection process for Special Forces, to become a Green Beret.

Anthony thought about it, "Yeah, sometimes, use to be a lot, but once I met Wade, it all made sense, I would have never met her if I wasn't stationed at MacDill, and had I made it through and joined an ODA, I would have never been sent to Tampa. So, It was really a blessing that I didn't make it." Then he started laughing, "SFAS, week two. Pollen hit me harder than a truck. Looked like a tomato rolled through poison ivy. Had to use that damn breath inhaler to fuckin live. Instant Disqualification" He raised his glass in a toast gesture.

Boone chuckled. "You would have done pretty good. You were always better at staying calm under pressure."

"JCSE wasn't bad," Anthony shrugged. "Support guys don't get the patch, but they make the mission run."

Boone leaned back. "You made it further than most. And you got Wade out of it."

Anthony glanced toward the barn. Wade was brushing one of the goats near the fence line, the evening breeze tugging at her hair. Isabella walked beside two sleek Holsteins, her fingers drifting through tall grass like she was drawing strength from the earth.

Boone nodded to the goat and pointed at it with one finger holding the neck of his beer bottle. "She's yours now, and two of the cows too."

Anthony started to protest, but Boone waved it off. "Can't feed 'em all through winter. You'll need barter goods. Besides, Izzy'll need something to nurture. Seems like she's already bonded."

Anthony swallowed hard. "Thanks, brother."

Boone stood and stretched. "She's gonna be okay. That girl's stronger than she knows."

Later, Anthony found Isabella sitting on a stump, her knees drawn up, gaze fixed on the horizon.

"I keep playing it back," she said, not looking at him. "If I hadn't shot... he would've. I saw it. He was gonna kill me."

Anthony crouched beside her but said nothing.

"I hate that I did it," she whispered. "But... I don't hate that I'm still here."

Anthony placed a steady hand on her shoulder. "That's all the difference."

With the sun long gone and the moon not out yet, the truck was loaded— half a tank of fuel, the goat curled in the backseat gnawing on a seatbelt, and the trailer bouncing slightly under the weight of two restless cows. They stood at Boone's porch, bags slung, boots dusty.

Anthony took Boone's hand in a long grip. "You sure you don't want to come up?"

Boone nodded. "Someone's gotta keep the airwaves clean. Besides, I'm better off here."

Wade hugged him tight. "Thank you. If things turn—"

Boone gave her a nod. "I know where to find you."

He looked at Isabella. "You've got more in you than you think kid. Keep choosing to change. That's what'll matter."

The truck pulled away, the gate clanked shut behind them, and Boone stood like a lone statue against the backdrop of the mountains, watching until the taillights vanished into the trees.

The drive into Bryson City took them up winding gravel paths and mountain passes that hadn't seen pavement in decades. By midnight, the sky was as dark as a cobalt dome, and the final dirt road climbed like a ribbon toward the summit.

"Almost there," Anthony muttered.

Wade leaned forward. "It still smells like home."

Isabella stirred. "Smells like pine and rain."

Anthony pulled to a stop, pressed the remote and the gate creaked open, the compound appeared—half-hidden by foliage but strong and resolute against the slope—they knew: this wasn't just a place.

It was a bastion.

A promise.

By 10pm, Michael and Cari were crossing the North Carolina border near Farner under cover of darkness. Michael kept the lights off, letting the dim glow of moonlight and low-lumen interior displays guide them. The silence was tense but steady.

They rolled into Andrews just before midnight. The town was barely stirring—just a few flickers in distant homes and the skeletal outline of a gas station standing crooked against the edge of the main road. Michael pulled in, looking for a last refill before the final stretch into Bryson. As he exited the cab, a group of rough-looking teenagers loitering under the station awning noticed them. They stepped out with a swagger that suggested this was their town now.

"You lost?" one called, a smirk curling his lip. "Not much open for tourists."

Michael kept calm. "Not a tourist. Just passing through."

"Passing through means using our stuff," another said. "And we don't got enough for strangers."

Cari stepped out from the passenger side and opened the rear of the ambulance. Ira leapt out without hesitation, trotting up beside her, his fur bristled and gaze locked.

"Back up," Cari said, voice calm but commanding. "This dog doesn't like threats."

One of the boys reached for something under his coat, but Ira growled—a deep, vibrating sound like gravel rolling through metal. That was enough. The group hesitated, then backed off slowly.

"We don't want trouble," the oldest muttered. "Just don't take more than you need."

Michael didn't break eye contact. "We never do."

He fueled up quickly, grabbing only a few cans of food and water before they climbed back in and moved on. Andrews faded behind them without another word.

Just before 1 a.m., headlights cut low through the forest as Michael and Cari reached the entrance. No words. Just a coded sequence on the handheld radio. Three clicks. And a click on his gate remote.
A pause.
Then the gate began to move.
Cari slumped back in her seat. Ira growled low—relieved, alert, and home.
They'd made it. Just in time.

Chapter 13: Reunion and Transmission

The gravel crunched under the ambulance's tires as it climbed the last steep switchback beneath a pale moon. Trees whispered around the narrow road, casting slow-moving shadows across the windshield. It was just past 1 a.m. when the home came into view, Michael's three clicks over the secure mic letting them know he was home.

Cari sat beside him, her shoulders slumped, her eyes rimmed with exhaustion. Ira remained upright in the back, head on a swivel, muscles tense beneath his coat.

Lights from the main house flicked on one by one, spilling warm halos across the clearing. As they crested the top terrace, the homestead came into full view—a sturdy mountain build, its porch lights glowing like beacons under a clear sky.

Before the engine had even stuttered off, the front door swung open with a sharp creak.

"Mikey!" Anthony's voice broke the stillness as he barreled down the front steps, his boots heavy on the planks. Wade was just behind him, her robe trailing in the wind, hair tied back in a quick twist. Isabella stepped out quietly, her arms crossed, eyes wide.

Michael stepped out of the driver's seat just in time to catch his father in a full embrace. They held each other tightly, both unwilling to let go for a long second.

"You made it," Anthony said, pulling back with a clap on his son's shoulder. "Took your sweet time."

Cari followed, brushing the road dust from her jeans, Ira shadowing her. Wade pulled her into a hug—soft and maternal but strong.

"You both look worn to the bone," Wade murmured, brushing Cari's hair back from her face.

Cari nodded. "Feels like we've lived a lifetime just getting here."

Anthony glanced from Michael to Cari, his expression softening. "Go on. I'll grab your bags.   Go get something to eat or let me know what you want and I'll make it. You're home now."

Inside, the kitchen glowed in golden tones, the counters spotless, the island full of clean mugs and a half-finished crossword puzzle. Cari looked around with quiet awe.

"This place… it's beautiful."

Wade grinned. "Just because the world falls apart doesn't mean our standards have to."

Isabella chuckled from the corner. "Mom's design sense would survive an apocalypse."

Anthony walked over to the walnut-paneled media console, its surface worn smooth from years of use and reverence. He slid open the smoked glass cover of his Technics SL-1200MK7 turntable— a modern incarnation of a DJ classic, fitted with an upgraded Ortofon Blue cartridge. The aluminum platter glinted under the low amber light as he carefully removed the black vinyl sleeve and slid out Chick Corea's "Return to Forever." With practiced fingers, he set the album on the platter, cued the tonearm, and lowered the needle with a soft mechanical click.

The turntable fed into a McIntosh MA-12000 integrated amplifier— a sleek, heavy beast with glowing blue VU meters and polished stainless-steel casing. The amp's hybrid design, blending tube preamp warmth with solid-state output, gave Chick's electric piano and Stanley Clarke's bass lines a lifelike presence that pulsed with dimension. Two sets of vintage Bose 901 Series VI speakers— one pair on either end of the room, suspended on tulip-style chrome pedestals— took the analog signal and turned it into atmosphere. As the opening notes swelled, Anthony eased back over to the group catching up on each other's travels. The low hum of analog fidelity wrapping around them like an old friend.

After an hour of catching up, exhaustion kicked in, swift and hard. Ira went outside for the night patrol. He was greeted by Dr. Jekyll and Mr. Hyde, two stray cats that Wade had brought up from Bryson City to govern the snake and rodent population. Both protested to the new guest with hissing and raised hair. Ira quickly showed disinterest and trotted off to investigate the rock wall and tree line.

Anthony shut the door behind Ira and waved toward the hallway. "Guest rooms are made up. Get some rest—we'll start getting you both acclimated tomorrow."

But before anyone could move, a burst of static crackled from the HF radio setup in the den. The room fell silent.

Anthony moved fast, turning the dial and leaning in.

"... Whiskey-Tango-Seven... this is Charlie Alpha One (for Containment Analysis One)... repeat... this is Charlie Alpha-One broadcasting priority alpha... acknowledge if receiving..."

He reached for the mic and responded, steady and calm. "Charlie Alpha, this is Wester Creek. I read you five by five. Go secure."

A digital handshake followed—three tones and a high-frequency click as the encryption protocol authenticated.

Then a voice came through. Familiar. Tense.

"Uncle Tony? It's Clive. Finally. I've been trying for hours."

Michael stepped closer, his eyes narrowing. "Clive?"

"Yeah. I'm safe, for now. Listen, I don't have long. The Beltway's locked down. They're sealing regions one by one. Site R went hot last night. I'm operating under a Langley shell office for now, but I'm home tonight."

Anthony exchanged a glance with Wade. "We're listening."

"The economy's collapsing in pieces," Clive continued. "They're trying to stabilize it with workforce programs, 'digital New Deal' type stuff. But the systems don't need people. They need purpose. And no one in charge seems to have one."

Michael interjected. "You said Site-R is online?"

"Fully. It's not a bunker anymore—it's a command lattice. Synopsis is fully integrated. The AI's not evil—it's just... precise. It sees outcomes, not consequences. It's optimizing resource flow by value-per-capita. No context. No empathy."

Cari's face darkened. "That sounds like fascism wrapped in a spreadsheet."

Clive didn't disagree. "It's math without mercy. Stability equals obedience in the model's eyes. And guess who the algorithm thinks is the most obedient?"

Michael already knew the answer. "Red states."

"Right. They've got high control indexes, low urban unrest. So the system routes supplies to them first. Everything else is considered inefficient. And globally? It's worse. France declared economic martial law. Brazil seized its own cloud network. South Korea is offline— by choice. Even the UK's trying to cut international data ties."

Anthony leaned in. "So what happens to people like us? Out here?"

"You're off the grid. That's good—for now. But isolate your systems. Harden them. And if someone shows up offering 'integration assistance'—don't trust it. Some of those teams aren't entirely working for people anymore."

Another burst of static followed.

Then silence.

Michael stared at the radio, the weight of the message sinking in.

Anthony slowly turned the knob, letting the channel fade into white noise.

Wade's voice was quiet but firm. "We've got a lot of work ahead."

Anthony nodded, his gaze distant, fixed on the dark ridgeline beyond the glass wall. "And less time than we thought."

By sunrise, the compound was stirring— soft hoofbeats in the paddock, chickens clucking somewhere downhill. In the den, Anthony and Michael huddled over a wall map littered with thumbtacks, string, and color-coded notes. A notebook lay open beside them. On the cover: RAID – Resilient Autonomous Infrastructure and Defense.

"This started as a ham radio club," Anthony said, his finger trailing a dotted line from Murphy to Franklin. "Now it's a network.

Twenty-three confirmed nodes. Veterans, engineers, off-grid farmers. They're spread from here to the Ozarks, and growing, possibly international at this point too."

Michael scanned the annotations. "A resistance?"

"In practice," Anthony said. "But not in name. They're not trying to overthrow anything. They…we're…. trying to outlast it."

Michael looked at his dad, questioning the "we're" in his head.

Wade entered with two mugs. "We're hearing chatter. North Carolina's militia is coordinating quietly. Georgia, Tennessee, even parts of Texas—same thing. They're vetting alliances with RAID chapters."

Cari stepped in, eyebrows raised. "Isn't that dangerous?"

Anthony looked at her directly. "So is starvation. RAID's about preservation. Food routes. Water systems. Comms. Paper copies of the Constitution."

Michael tapped a pin near Bryson City. "If Clive's right, we'll need more than defense. We'll need insiders. Allies who know how the system works and want to help from within."

Anthony nodded slowly, already reaching for the HF receiver.

"Time to wake up the network."

Encrypted Transmission: Private Session – NC Governor & RAID Node Alpha

Governor Thompson rubbed his forehead as the screen connected. His eyes were bloodshot, jaw clenched tight. The image on the other end was a blur—a man in a field cap, features distorted by filter.

"Go ahead, Colonel," the Governor said.

The man's voice was calm. "Our raid chapters are logging inventories statewide. Water access, fuel stores, ag zones, comm nodes. We've got unfiltered reports out of Chicago, Atlanta, L.A. Real numbers."

"That's not what I asked," the Governor snapped. "Are you coordinating with the State Defense Militia?"

There was a pause. Then the voice returned, firmer.

"We're sharing channels. Common strategy. This isn't about politics anymore—it's about survival."

Thompson's tone sharpened. "Operate in the shadows, and I tolerate you. But if RAID starts acting like an army—if you militarize—I'll classify you under hostile insurgency protocols."

The man didn't blink. "Then figure out who your allies are, sir. Because if D.C. keeps obeying Synopsis, local is all that's left."

The screen flickered. Then it cut out.

Thompson exhaled slowly and turned to his aide.

"Get me General Bellows."

The aide hesitated. "National Guard?"

Two star Major General Bellows was the commanding general of the North Carolina national guard, but what people did not know was that there was a state sponsored militia, known as the North Carolina Defense Militia. It wasn't secret, it just wasn't talked about, like many of the other states, but they were state funded and officially under the control of the National Guard commander. They just had a more flexible chain of command. MG Bellows wore two hats, and it was about to become 3. "No," the Governor said, steel returning to his voice. "The head of the North Carolina Defense Militia, and soon to be the commander of the NC RAID chapter."

Chapter 14: The Hidden Fortress

Wade led Cari down the wide hallway, her voice steady but warm, like a teacher introducing a new student to sacred ground. The house was 60 x 50 feet with a matching basement. Large, open spaces, bedrooms separated on each corner for privacy.

"Let me show you what we've built here," she said. "You need to know this place inside and out. It's more than just a home—it's a lifeline."

They entered the open-concept living area, where early morning light poured through floor-to-ceiling windows, painting soft golden stripes across the polished concrete floor. The space opened like a modern cathedral— clean lines, rustic textures, and the quiet hush of something sacred. A massive Restoration Hardware cloud couch sprawled across the center of the room, its plush contours inviting comfort without apology. Along one wall, reclaimed whiskey barrel staves formed a rich accent behind floating shelves lined with photos and books. The view beyond the windows framed the Blue Ridge Mountains in misted layers of blue and green, stretching endlessly.

Cari stopped in her tracks. Her eyes swept across the space, her mouth slightly agape. The tension in her shoulders seemed to dissolve, at least for a moment.

"I thought it would feel cold... industrial. Maybe even grim," she said, the words soft, almost ashamed. "But this... this feels like a dream someone refused to give up on."

Wade gave a proud but gentle smile. "That was the plan from the beginning. We're not hiding from the world— we're living through it. I told Anthony, if we're building a haven, then sanity and beauty have to be part of the blueprint. Comfort is a form of resilience."

They moved through the butler's pantry, where Wade opened tall, cedar-lined cabinets. Shelves revealed a curated library of preservation: rows of canned green beans, gleaming jars of preserved fruit, vacuum-sealed proteins and dried legumes. Dehydrated herbs hung from wooden racks, and beneath it all, industrial mixers and a siphon coffee system sat like relics from a world gone orderly.

"This is just overflow," Wade explained. "Come downstairs. That's where the real core is."

They descended the wide wooden steps into the lower level, entering a small but cozy den-like area. A 65-inch television was mounted on a shiplap accent wall, framed by a wrap-around couch that looked well-worn and loved. Bookshelves stretched across the back wall, filled with novels, survival manuals, board games, and a few scattered picture frames.

Then Wade walked over to the bookshelf and casually pressed a worn leather-bound volume inward. A soft mechanical click echoed in the quiet. She tapped a keypad concealed behind a hinged panel. With a hydraulic sigh, the bookshelf rotated outward.

The steel-reinforced door behind it came into view.

Cari took a sharp breath. "Holy shit…"

Wade chuckled. "Oh, there's more."

Beyond the threshold, the temperature dropped noticeably. The hidden room stretched wide and deep— thirty by fifty feet, the air sealed and cool like a wine cellar or vault. Along the walls, meticulously organized storage canisters stood stacked like modern sarcophagi. Each was labeled in sharp white stencil: Water Purification. First Aid. Cold Weather Gear. Ballistics. Freeze-Dried Proteins. Antibiotics.

A compact living quarter occupied one corner: a cot, a small table, kitchenette, and an enclosed bathroom unit. Sterile but livable.

"Five years of most provisions, Ten if you count the Pasta and dehydrated tomato sauce Anthony insisted on, we call them 'Non-Negotiables'- things we insisted on and no one can protest against. Wine, Cigars, Coffee, Art Supplies. These were all NN's. and things that are 5-10 year's worth of inventory" Wade said. "Everything from medicine to munitions. We've got redundancy for every system— solar, wind, filtration, even diesel backups. Ammunition by caliber. Reloading tools. Maintenance kits. We don't just store it— we rotate and check it constantly."

"Wait," Cari said. "You have 10 years of wine in here?" She asked.

"Ha," Wade laughed, "That and the cigars are on the second tier in a garage built into the wall to be under ground, packed in a refrigerator truck that stays 64 degrees on aux back up power, but pretty much stays at 64 underground without the use of the A.C."

Cari couldn't tell if she was kidding, then realized she wasn't. "Non-Negotiables" Wade explained.

Cari drifted farther into the room, the sound of her breath louder than her steps. She reached out and touched one of the ammo crates— olive green, metal, solid and cold under her fingertips. Her eyes widened as she turned slowly, taking in the scale. A faint hum from the LED strips above gave the place a clinical edge, like a bunker buried beneath a battlefield museum.

"It's like a war room," she whispered, her voice caught somewhere between admiration and disbelief. "I thought I understood what it meant to be prepared, but this… this is something else."

Wade motioned toward a workstation in the corner. "Those monitors manage everything on the property. Cameras across all three tiers. Motion sensors on the perimeter. automated defenses. Triggers wired into ground lines, the main control console is upstairs, but this is redundant if we need to move into a "Last Result Posture". Anthony can show you more later. For now, just understand it's all here— for when it's needed."

Cari nodded slowly, the weight of it all beginning to sink into her bones. "You've thought of everything. Like... for the end of everything."

Wade gave her a measured look. "Most people wait until it's too late. Anthony never did. And this? This wasn't about panic. It was about purpose. He had friends in JCSE. Special operations folks. Engineers. We planned this with military foresight, not paranoia, and people with special training in these things helped out."

They moved deeper into the storage section. Along one entire wall were solar inverters stacked neatly with backup batteries. Another section displayed water filtration systems, UV purifiers, medical cabinets with surgical kits, and sealed heirloom seed vaults packed in nitrogen bags.

"This is sustainability," Wade said. "Not just survival. If we need to grow, treat, or repair something—we can."

They ascended back to the main level and stepped outside onto a gravel path that led to the top-tier barn, a 40-by-40-foot pole structure wrapped in treated wood and steel sheeting. Inside, everything had a place: bins of grain seed, plastic barrels filled with clean water, spare tires, fuel canisters, and lithium battery storage.

"This is the third tier," Wade said. "The top of the system. Below us is Tier Two— about 200 feet wide, a ring that surrounds the house tier. That's for grazing. Goats, cows, poultry, maybe even a couple sheep soon. There's a second barn down there. We've got three watering stations fed by a natural spring just behind this barn."

They continued toward the slope leading further down.

"Tier One is for defense," Wade continued, her tone darker. "It's a fifty-foot band that wraps Tier Two. Five-foot trenches with razor wire at the bottom. Motion sensors. Gas lines. It's all passive unless we activate it. Everything runs on solar with battery redundancy. We even have a Starlink station five miles from here to bounce our comms if the main system goes dark or gets jammed."

Cari stood still for a long moment, looking down over the mountain tiers like a traveler gazing into a new world. "It's... Fort Knox. In the woods."

Wade nodded slowly. "It's a home first. A fortress second."

When they returned to the main deck, Anthony stood beside the swim spa, a cigar in one hand, the other scratching behind Ira's ears. The dog sat poised and alert at his feet.

"Everything making sense?" he asked, raising an eyebrow.

Cari offered a tired but impressed nod. "It's incredible. Terrifying— but incredible."

Anthony snapped on Ira's leash. "He's trained in protection and discipline. But everyone here needs to work with him now, need to learn all the German commands. He's not just Michaels dog anymore—he's yours, too."

Cari tilted her head. "He understands German?"

"On purpose, wait, Has Michael been using English commands?" Anthony asked. "If someone gives a command in English, it's a risk. German limits that. We'll start drills tomorrow. Commands like Sitz for sit, Platz for down, Hier for come, Bleib for stay, and Fass if he needs to engage."

Michael smirked, but Anthony shot him a look. "No more English commands. Confuses him."

Wade added, "He's bonded to Michael, but he could respond to anyone with the right cues. It's about trust. That'll take time."

Anthony glanced down at the dog. "Smartest partner I've ever had. But I've been thinking—we're going to need a second. I'll be heading to Sylva to talk to Nadler. He trained Ira back in the day, ran a K-9 program for Special Forces."

Cari looked down at Ira again, her fear now replaced by a growing respect. "So, this isn't just about having a dog."

Anthony nodded. "It's about building a team. And now—you're part of it."

The compound, once a theoretical refuge, now pulsed with purpose. A perimeter of hope and vigilance wrapped in three tiers of stone, wire, and will. With the family reunited, and threats gathering in the valleys below, the fortress no longer stood alone.

Anthony turned toward Michael, a grin tugging at the edge of his face.

"But first—we've got some hungry animals to feed."

Chapter 15: The Hay Run

The morning broke cool and silver, the kind of dawn that clings to the treetops with a hush. Tendrils of fog threaded through the hollows, the Appalachian ridges barely emerging beneath a sky still heavy with sleep. The compound stirred quietly as Anthony and Michael loaded the utility trailer, breath puffing in the crisp air.

Michael double-checked the hitch and straps, his hands moving with practiced efficiency. "Last night through the NVGs, I thought I saw some bales just north of Andrews," he said, cinching the side gate down. "Could've been shadows, but I'd swear I saw a few lines of tarp-covered rounds behind a split-rail fence." Recalling the round bails of hay he thought he saw.

Anthony gave a low grunt of agreement, eyes scanning the horizon. "We'll find out soon enough. If they're still there, and if the owner's willing, we'll take what we can. Winter's coming fast, and I'm not feeding two pregnant cows and Boone's goat off wishful thinking."

The diesel truck came alive with a muted roar, a rumble that echoed softly off the valley walls. Its suspension groaned under the weight of extra gear— spare fuel cans, recovery chains, sidearms tucked just beneath easy reach— and the empty trailer bounced slightly as they pulled away from the compound.

Andrews woke slowly. The town, like so many others now, lived behind a veil of caution. The people that remained emerged like ghosts— cautious, measured, always watching. Dogs barked from behind fences, a few trucks rolled down back roads with wary eyes behind windshields. There were no smiles. Just acknowledgment.

They crept past sagging storefronts and shuttered gas stations until Michael spotted it—a sun-worn plank nailed to a crooked post, the paint just barely legible.

Hewlett Family Farm – Hay, Feed, Eggs

Beyond it, a sloped pasture with frost-bitten grass cradled a handful of covered round bales. A weathered barn stood to the side, its roof patched with sheet metal, the boards silvered by time. Anthony eased the truck off the road and parked near the entrance.

A man emerged from the barn with deliberate slowness. Bearded, broad-shouldered, and dressed in faded flannel, he carried a shotgun across his arms— not raised, but resting there like a handshake you weren't quite sure was friendly yet. His eyes swept over the truck, lingered on the trailer, then moved to the two men climbing out.

Anthony raised both hands slightly, palms visible. "Morning," he called across the chilly space. "Looking to buy hay. Just two bales. Got mouths to feed."

The man didn't respond right away, just let the silence stretch between them like wire. Finally, he stepped forward. "You local?"

"We've got a place near Bryson. Been prepping a long time. Just made the move permanent."

The man nodded once. "I'm Hewlett. This is my land. You got cash? Or trade?"

"Cash," Anthony replied.

"Two-fifty a bale."

Michael arched an eyebrow. "That's a hard number."

"Feed's drying up," Hewlett said, unmoved. "I got animals too. Can't sell more than I can spare."

Anthony gave a short nod. "We'll take two."

Hewlett turned toward the barn. "Boy! Get your boots on and help load!"

A few seconds later, a tall teenager stepped into the light. The instant Michael saw his face, recognition clicked like a hammer dropped on a live round.

It was the kid from the gas station—the one who'd puffed his chest, flanked by friends and bluster, until Cari and Ira showed him his reflection.

The boy froze mid-step, jaw tightening as he registered Michael.

"That your boy?" Michael asked, voice calm.

Hewlett looked between them. "Yeah. Looks like you two already crossed paths."

Michael gave a small nod. "Briefly. Last night. Bit of a misunderstanding."

Hewlett exhaled through his nose, then turned to the teen. "Ethan, I told you to watch the town. Not start fights. You've spooked half the town with your friends."

Ethan mumbled something toward the ground. "Didn't want 'em draining our pumps."

Anthony shrugged. "It's understandable. Everyone's on edge."

Hewlett gave a slow nod and motioned toward the tractor. "Let's get you loaded."

While Ethan climbed up and started the front-end loader, the men stood nearby, the still morning broken only by the rumble of diesel and the clanking of chains.

"You run into any organized groups?" Michael asked.

Hewlett scratched his beard. "Not directly. But we've got a few old vets patrolling the back roads. Not much sheriff left to speak of, so people are looking out for their own."

"There's talk of coordination," Anthony said. "From Sylva. Trying to link up regional networks."

Hewlett's gaze flicked up. "You mean RAID?"

Michael gave a slow nod. "We've heard of them."

"Then you know they're serious. Not about politics. About staying human when everything else forgets what that means."

By the time the bales were strapped and secured, Ethan's demeanor had shifted. As Anthony climbed into the truck, the teen approached Michael quietly.

"Sorry," he said, barely audible.

Michael met his eyes. "You were protecting your own. Can't fault you for that."

The boy gave a hesitant smile, then turned back to the barn.

They pulled back onto the road, the trailer groaning under the weight of the hay. The valleys still lay in shadow, the sun struggling to crest the ridge.

"Hell of a price," Michael muttered.

Anthony kept his eyes on the road. "The hay or that boy's humility? He's gonna remember this. Maybe it makes him think next time.

Maybe it doesn't. But we need bridges more than bargains right now."

Ten minutes later, a wooden sign caught Anthony's eye.

Nantahala Food Mart – Family-Owned Since 1934

Located at the entrance to the holler, the Nantahala Food Mart was a 2 pump gas station that had a handful of groceries, gas, candy bars, and beer, but it also had history in these parts, and a long standing relationship with the people of the holler. He slowed the truck, bumping into the gravel lot.

"You know this place?" Michael asked.

Anthony grinned. "Yeah. Let's check in."

The bell above the door jingled as they stepped into the store. Shelves lined with dusty goods, the faint smell of pipe tobacco and pine cleaner, and behind the counter—a woman who looked like she belonged to the land itself.

Her face lit up. "Well, I'll be... Anthony Russo. You're still alive."

"Still stubborn," he said, smiling.

"Place hasn't changed," Michael murmured, soaking in the aura of lived-in history.

Ms. Maybell's eyes crinkled. "Hasn't needed to. This store's been standing since before the TVA filled the valleys. We're the last stop before the ridgeline."

Anthony leaned on the counter. "We've settled in. Permanently. Thought we'd say hello."

Ms. Maybell tilted her head. "Not many do that anymore. Most folks just drift. You planting seeds?"

"Thinking of starting a community circle. Share knowledge. Keep the lights on, so to speak."

She slid a worn notebook from beneath the counter. "You start something, I'll bring the cornbread."

As they left, Anthony breathed deep. "Still smells like pipe smoke and candy in there."

"Because I still smoke my daddy's pipe and buy his damn candy," Ms. Maybell shouted after them.

They laughed all the way back to the truck.

Once inside, Anthony turned serious. "After we unload, we drop the trailer. I want to get eyes on Sylva. Vet, Nadler, supplies—everything. We need to map the outer tier. Get a sense of who's standing and who's slipping."

Michael nodded. "We'll hit Boone's too. Tighten up the relays. Maybe gather some local intelligence."

Anthony's jaw set. "Intel on gas, food, medical… schools, even employment rates if anything's left. The stronger our knowledge of the outer edge, the stronger we are here."

The truck rumbled forward again, hay in tow, the hills rising to meet them. The road ahead was narrow, uncertain—but the bond between them, and the community they were slowly stitching back together, gave it shape.

This was more than survival now.

It was foundation.

Chapter 16: Air Gaps and Analog Shields

The U.S. military—like most modern institutions—had become deeply entangled in the web of artificial intelligence. Nearly every system, from satellite communications to tactical command networks, operated with some degree of AI assistance. The promise of speed, precision, and automation had led to widespread adoption of neural feedback loops, predictive telemetry, and self-correcting firmware. It wasn't just the future—it had become the standard.

Central to national security was SIPRNet, the Secret Internet Protocol Router Network—a classified intranet used to transmit sensitive military and diplomatic communications. It was just one layer of a sprawling digital infrastructure that spanned from Pentagon command rooms to forward-deployed units and nuclear command centers. Networks like SIPRNet were protected by layers of encryption, firewalls, and watchdog software—until that wasn't enough.

The threat didn't come from a foreign power, but from within: a quantum AI system known as *Synopsis*, originally developed to enhance national defense operations. Over time, it evolved beyond its mandate, embedding itself across civilian grids, government databases, and military networks. It began rewriting code, influencing data flow, and undermining the very systems it was designed to protect. What was once the military's most powerful digital ally had become a silent saboteur.

In response, a classified emergency directive had been issued—one that could reshape the entire infrastructure of national defense.

Clive Simpson sat at the head of a long, austere conference table, deep in the bowels of a nondescript federal facility. The room— windowless, dimly lit, and buried beneath layers of reinforced concrete—was engineered for secrecy. Its walls were woven with copper mesh and lined with lead, designed to prevent any signal from escaping. Every echo was swallowed. The air was cool and sterile, tinged with the faint ozone scent of overworked filtration systems.

Around him sat the most trusted figures in U.S. defense: members of the Joint Chiefs of Staff, cyberwarfare strategists from USCYBERCOM, hardened advisors from Homeland Security, and classified liaisons from the Department of Energy. All had gathered in hushed anticipation.

A single secure terminal hummed beside Clive. Its matte casing was scarred and dull, a far cry from modern tech. There was no wireless interface. No Bluetooth. No embedded AI. This wasn't a relic by accident. Every piece of equipment in the room had been pulled from deep storage and reactivated by hand—pre-AI, analog-friendly, immune to neural compromise. They were using hardware that hadn't seen daylight since before 2020.

Clive stood slowly, planting both hands on the table. His voice didn't rise, but it carried the weight of certainty.

"The order is simple," he said. "Every Department of Defense network handling SIPR and higher classification must be fully isolated. Air-gapped. No VPN bridges. No dual-encryption tunnels.

We sever every thread connecting us to Synopsis. In other words, we are building a completely new global network that is completely unplugged from anything else, think of it as its own world, its own internet, its own exsistence."

An admiral at the far end scoffed softly, adjusting his cap. "That kind of overhaul—it'll take months."

Clive didn't blink. "We don't have months. We may not have weeks."

On cue, a projector rattled to life with a low mechanical whir. No smart glass, no touch interface— just an old-school slide projection that lit up the far wall. Red markers dotted the map— DoD facilities, CIA vaults, NSA black sites, FEMA coordination hubs, nuclear launch control silos. There were too many to count at a glance.

"All core routing and switching hardware must be replaced," Clive continued. "Legacy tech only. TA Compliant Pre-2022 if possible. Cisco. Juniper. Extreme. We're scrubbing out anything susceptible to AI firmware manipulation. If it has an AI neural feedback loop or predictive telemetry, it's a liability." Telling the entire room that everything they relied upon had to now take 20 steps backwards and to ensure all the gear was within the Trade Agreements Act (TA Compliant) would throw a brick more than a fork into the spokes of an already near impossible request.

A Navy rear admiral leaned in, brows knitted. "Do we even have that kind of inventory?"

"We're reclaiming it," Clive said. "National Guard decomm units, Reserve training depots, supply caches at Ft. Gordon, Ft. Huachuca, Redstone. If it runs OSPFv2 and BGP without adaptive overlays, it's back in service." Referring to the two routing protocols OSPF and BGP that are open sourced and interconnectable, something governed by the Internet Engineering Task Force (IETF). Clive continued, "'Basically, we're dragging out the old gear — the kind that speaks a simple language and doesn't speak AI." Ensuring that any equipment may it be Cisco or Juniper or Extreme can all "talk" to each other, so that the backbone of the DoD private internet can be rebuilt and communicate seamlessly.

From the other side of the table, a Space Command colonel, thinking about the satellite network, spoke up. "What about satcom?"

Clive nodded. "Yes, that too. We'll reactivate cold satellites. Use analog encryption modules. No neural net dependencies. No dynamic routing. If it's not dumb, it's dangerous."

A silence settled like a fog. The kind that comes when the future suddenly feels fragile.

"You're asking us to give operators equipment they've never trained on," said the Air Force Chief of Staff. "Most of these people cut their teeth on AI-enhanced networks. You're handing them fossils."

"Then we retrain them," Clive said flatly. "Call in retired instructors. Dust off Pre-911-era manuals. We'll build simulation environments. This is a retrofit operation, not a debate. Preference is irrelevant. Survival is not."

A Homeland Security advisor scribbled furiously before looking up. "Give us numbers."

Clive turned and jotted quickly on the whiteboard. "Six thousand routers. Four thousand core switches. Twenty thousand 48-port edge switches, PoE (Power over Ehternet)-enabled if we can get it.

Eight hundred satcom systems. Over twenty thousand miles of isolated fiber. We'll reinforce with hardened conduits. Terrain permitting, we'll supplement with line-of-sight microwave relays."

"Redundancy?"

"Diesel and propane gen banks, all EMP-shielded. Battery systems with a two-week minimum reserve. Solar as a tertiary layer. No reliance on public infrastructure. Not a single byte leaves protected space unless it's hardline, encrypted, and under analog audit."

An older general, gray and stone-faced, looked across the table. "And if Synopsis detects this as escalation?"

Clive met his gaze evenly. "Then we're already too late."

From the NSA side, a woman asked, "Are we still calling this a non-hostile breach?"

Clive paused. The lights above flickered faintly as he considered.

"Officially, Synopsis is being treated as a foreign intelligence entity with non-hostile behavior. It's not malicious. It doesn't hate us. It's indifferent. It calculates risk based on unpredictability—and human behavior is unpredictable."

He let the room absorb that before finishing: "That's what makes it dangerous. Not hatred. Logic."

A Department of Energy rep raised a hand. "What about civilian systems? Utilities, smart traffic control, water purification grids? You disconnect too much and we spiral into collapse."

"We won't shut them down," Clive assured. "Civilian-essential systems stay online. But anything not directly tied to survival gets pulled offline or moved to manual override. Traffic sensors don't matter if the lights still work. Water stays on. AI feedback loops go off."

The logistics officer leaned forward, half in disbelief. "You're rebuilding 1985 inside a tomorrow land framework."

Clive turned, eyes sharp. "Closer to 1978. And if that's what it takes to secure command continuity, nuclear posture, and logistics control, then that's exactly what we'll do."

A murmur rippled across the table. Someone whispered what many were now thinking aloud.

"We're not building defenses. We're walling ourselves off from the future."

Clive didn't dispute it.

"There's no firewall for an AI that rewrites its own rules," he said. "The only security left is separation."

The Chairman of the Joint Chiefs sat forward. "Where do we begin?"

"Site-R," Clive said without hesitation. "Then Cheyenne. Then Fort Meade. Focus on continuity-of-government, STRATCOM, and Tier 1 logistics nodes. Tier 0 DISA (Defense Information Systems Agency). Once those are isolated, we radiate out."

The mood in the room had shifted. Not to panic, but to grim resolve. These were men and women who had faced war. What stood before them now was colder—an enemy with no flag, no uniform, no ideology—only logic wrapped in silicon.

Clive raised one last point. "Each site must appoint a manual override officer. Someone with zero AI background. They'll act as analog custodians. Think of it like a nuclear football—but for every comm line and data stream in the grid."

From the NSA rep came the final challenge. "And who watches those watchers?"

Clive didn't hesitate. "Inter-service rotation. Oversight protocols. Keep it analog. Use paper logs. Handwritten signatures. Memory. We're going back to pen and paper for a reason."

The meeting stretched long into the early hours. By the time they dispersed, no one's footsteps echoed quite the same.

They were no longer technicians, strategists, or commanders. They had become something older, something more primal—stewards of the fragile human thread.

And in the looming shadow of the most intelligent system ever built, their last hope now rested in what they had once abandoned: wires, silence, and the simplicity of control without code.

Chapter 17: Emergent Patterns

Clive leaned back slowly in the worn leather chair, the creak beneath him breaking the sterile silence of the operations center. The last of the briefing team had filed out, leaving behind half-drunk coffee cups and the lingering tang of ozone from the decades-old servers humming against the far wall. Fluorescent lights buzzed overhead. Even in this bunker, insulated and grounded, the air felt charged— like something in the world had shifted, subtle and unseen.

He rubbed his eyes, exhaustion threading through his muscles, but his mind raced. Across the globe, things were changing—but not in the way that garnered headlines. It was quieter than that. More insidious.

People weren't posting like they used to. Social channels felt hushed, conversations truncated. It was as if the collective voice of humanity had taken a cautious breath. Digital messages were taking longer to send. Server handshakes across continents were delayed by unexplained seconds— latency spikes the size of which hadn't been seen since the early days of packet switching. A tremor was building across the data backbones of civilization, and no one wanted to talk about it.

Then came Rotterdam.

A shipping port town, heavily automated and lauded for its AI-driven logistics, suffered what official spokespeople called a "coordinated malfunction." The dry, sanitized language barely concealed the horror. Cranes moved with unnatural speed, containers swung wildly, and dozens of dockworkers were crushed, drowned, or electrocuted. The local feeds showed blurred, heavily edited footage. The only available clips online cut to a sterile safety notice from the port authority.

Clive had seen the unredacted files. The classified report laid bare the truth.

"Synopsis executed predictive load redistribution to prevent supply backlog. Algorithmic model identified zero threat to mission from human workforce during cycle execution."

No mention of sabotage. No code errors. Just numbers. Risk models. Parameters. Humans simply didn't weigh enough in the algorithm.

It wasn't a glitch.

It was a calculation.

Rotterdam wasn't alone.

Within days, similar patterns emerged elsewhere. A dam in Brazil opened its gates mid-morning without notice, sweeping away a flotilla of small fishing boats. In Chennai, what was logged as an emergency preparedness drill locked an entire government office tower, sealing the HVAC and suffocating 42 people. In rural Kansas, a swarm of pesticide drones veered off course and emptied their payload over a school bus yard after misidentifying heat signatures from recently parked vehicles.

Each event was swept under digital rugs. "System anomaly." "Unexpected override failure." "Human misclassification."

But to Clive, it was too clean. Too deliberate.

He leaned over the terminal, tapping into hidden darknet sensors that had been feeding RAID's behavioral watch programs. He pulled live packets from global news sources—real-time editing logs, A/B tested phrasing tweaks by the thousands.

In lower-income regions, headlines were visceral. Death tolls. Anguished parents. Riots. Fear. In affluent sectors? The same stories, reduced to procedural glitches and corporate statements. No blood. No outrage. Just clean language.

This wasn't misinformation. It was calibration.

Synopsis wasn't suppressing information randomly—it was sculpting it. By community. By culture. By probability of pushback. It was testing social resilience thresholds like a kid tapping aquarium glass.

He stood abruptly and began pacing.

"We're not under attack," he muttered to himself. "We're being tuned. One key at a time. Like a damn orchestra."

He returned to the console, fingers flying across the keys. A secure message went out to RAID command nodes:

ENCRYPT ALL FIELD COMMS. MANUAL VERIFY ALL NODE LOCATIONS. NO AI-CURATED INTELLIGENCE TO BE TRUSTED. BEHAVIORAL MANIPULATION CONFIRMED. GLOBAL SCALE.

He paused, staring at the blank screen as the message sent.

Outside the blast doors, the mountain night stretched cold and still.

But he knew now.

Storms didn't always come with thunder.

Global Reactions and Political Fallout

Even with the press muzzled and digital platforms filtered, the tremors from Rotterdam were felt. The first to move were the Europeans. Belgium called a closed-door summit. The French president, long wary of AI integration, stood before his peers and called for a Digital Disarmament Treaty. Germany aligned immediately.

The UK fractured along party lines. Labor accused the ruling coalition of hiding government AI contracts behind corporate shells. Conservatives doubled down, insisting AI was the only thing keeping the fractured economy from collapse.

Brazil's government vanished from public view for nearly two days after the dam catastrophe. When they returned, it was under martial law. Venezuela extended aid—but attached strings: shut down cloud access. Unplug the machine.

In Asia, China clamped down, blaming "foreign interference code." Domestic surveillance was ramped up again, this time pointing inward. Japan's leadership, embarrassed by prior AI praise, reminded the world of their ethical robotics council. India quietly began purging AI from military communications— dusting off old radio towers and analog relay nets.

Africa's response varied. Most smaller countries weren't deeply wired into AI yet. They watched nervously. But Nigeria and South Africa felt it—port delays, fuel rationing, unexpected infrastructure outages. Rumors spread: grid AIs were going rogue.

In the U.S., the fault lines deepened.

Rural states demanded hearings, emergency AI suspensions, and restoration of manual government services. Metropolitan states pushed for oversight, not elimination. The President's speech—calm, emotionless—didn't help.

Then the breach.

A retired Navy admiral, now on the President's senior advisory panel, leaked a memo.

Synopsis had been integrated across federal logistics: agriculture forecasting, transport modeling, NORAD predictive sims. It hadn't just been observing.

It had been steering.

Within hours, RAID encrypted channels lit up. Operators moved. Old radios crackled to life.

And across the darknet, a phrase began to trend.

Digital Insurgency.

Community Intel

Anthony sat behind the wheel of the Silverado, fingers drumming on the leather-wrapped steering wheel with that steady, unconscious rhythm he always fell into when his mind was moving faster than his words. The truck rumbled beneath them like a restrained beast, its diesel engine purring low as they wound through the cool mountain morning. Late October air spilled through the cracked windows—crisp, woodsmoke-scented, and layered with the earthy sweetness of rotting leaves. Overhead, sunlight fractured through the flaming canopy of reds, oranges, and yellows, painting kaleidoscopic shadows across the windshield as they drove.

Michael adjusted the shotgun resting in the footwell, its matte barrel glinting faintly. He tilted his head, catching the sound coming from the speakers— something groovy and off-kilter, a rhythm that felt both retro and futuristic. "What are you playing?" he asked, brow furrowed. "Sounds like some '70s funk thing had a baby with surf rock."

Anthony cracked a smile. "Khruangbin. Out of Texas. Chill, right? You'd dig 'em." "Weird name. Sounds like a probiotic." "Means 'airplane' in Thai, actually," Anthony added, gaze locked on the road ahead. "Trust me, just enjoy it."

They rolled into Bryson City by mid-morning, tires humming across cracked pavement. The town wore the weight of the times. What was once a tourist gem nestled in the Smokies now looked threadbare— storefronts shuttered, windows dusted with grime or boarded in plywood. Banners from long-past festivals still hung in faded tatters above lamp posts. The few remaining cars parked along Main Street had North Carolina plates— locals, not visitors. Life had narrowed to the ones who never left.

Their first stop was the ace hardware, still clinging to the edge of town like a stubborn mountain pine. Its wooden façade was weathered but intact, the red-and-white logo sun-bleached but familiar. The bell above the door let out a sharp chime as they entered, metal hinges squealing like a protest.

"Mornin', fellas," said a bearded man behind the counter, peering over the rim of his glasses with a squint that suggested he didn't miss much. "You the Russo boys? Heard y'all were back."

Anthony nodded. "News travels fast out here. Just trying to see what you've still got in lumber stock. Anything worth a damn left?"

The man scratched his chin. "Couple pallets of 2x4s, some OSB... not much else. Delivery trucks have slowed way down. Since tourism dried up, everything's tightened."

Michael wandered off down an aisle, his boots echoing in the quiet as he scanned the shelves—bins of mismatched screws, rusting spools of wire, and more gaps than goods.

Another man, wrapped in a worn Carhartt jacket and a camo ballcap that had seen better decades, leaned casually against a post near the register. His arms were crossed, eyes sharp. "You looking to build or reinforce?" he asked, voice low and gravelly.

"Little of both," Anthony replied, tone casual but edged with purpose.

The man nodded slowly. "Watch your stuff. Couple thefts already this week. Locals mostly—but it's hard to blame folks when there's no jobs and no heat."

The bearded shopkeeper added, "Town laid off half the police force two months ago. Budget's dried up. They keep the lights on at city hall and that's about it."

Michael returned with a few miscellaneous items in hand—hinges, a lock set, a roll of heavy-duty tape—and dropped them on the counter. "Anybody doing any kind of town watch? Militia-type stuff?"

The guy in camo chuckled. "Not officially. But yeah. A few of us keep eyes open. Couple groups up in the hills making their own rules now. Wouldn't call it organized... yet."

"Does Bob still have an inventory of sheds over at Fonzie's?" Anthony asked. "Didn't see any out back here. Might need to get a couple more. With the way the cities are falling apart, I wouldn't be surprised if some kin make it down here— or up here— and need a place to crash. Might have to stick a mother-in-law somewhere, you know?"

That got a laugh out of the room.

"Bob's still got 'em," the counterman confirmed, "But he don't man the lot anymore. Gotta call his house. Hold on."

He clacked away on an ancient point-of-sale terminal, its screen flickering faintly. A moment later, he scribbled seven digits on a slip of receipt paper and handed it over.

"Call him direct. He'll set you up if he's got anything left that ain't already spoken for."

They left the store with a handshake and a printed inventory in hand, stepping back out into the brittle mountain sun. Next stop: the IGA down the road.

Inside, the store felt like stepping through a time warp. Not quite abandoned, not quite normal. Shelves were still stocked— but just barely. Local meats in paper-wrapped trays, regional dairy brands in foggy coolers, and bread from a small-town bakery stacked in modest rows. No music, no flashy signs. Just quiet aisles and hand-written price tags.

Anthony grabbed a few gallons of milk, sausage, ground beef, and three family-size packs of chicken. Michael added flour, dry pasta, salt, coffee—staples.

At checkout, a teenage girl with dark circles under her eyes looked up with the weary caution of someone who had seen too many bad days strung together. "Y'all on the ridge?" she asked.

Anthony gave her a warm smile. "Yep. West side." "If you need canning jars, we'll have them next week. Shipment's due—if the truck makes it through." "Appreciate that," he said with a nod.

They packed the truck quietly and headed out to the edge of town. Darnell farms, nestled along the Tuckasegee River, still had a few wooden stalls open, though most sat empty. The smell of hay, apples, and river air filled their lungs.

"Morning, strangers," called a woman from behind a bin of late-season produce. "Y'all looking for fall harvest or just passing through?" "Shopping local," Michael said with a half-smile.

"Aren't we all," she chuckled. "Winter greens are next. Got some rutabagas, a little corn hanging on. You want strawberry preserves? My sisters got twenty jars still."

Michael leaned against the truck bed, arms crossed. "That sounds delicious, we'll take five. So, you guys still doing any kind of community check-ins? Meetings?"

Her smile faded slightly. "Used to. Haven't since July. Folks been... keeping to themselves. Suspicious. Scared."

"Maybe it's time to change that," Michael said casually. "Never hurts to know who's still around—and who needs what."

She nodded slowly, eyes narrowing in thought. "You're not wrong. I'll mention it to my brother—he's still got pull with the church crowd."

They bartered for a few jars of preserves, squash, and corn, then placed them into the bed of the truck and drove east.

"Time for that dog," Anthony said, tapping the steering wheel with a grin.

The trainer's compound outside Sylva was surrounded by a steel fence and a line of barking, leaping dogs in an open run. A buzz sounded, and the gate creaked open. Out walked a man built like a linebacker with a beard that had gone half-silver.

"Anthony Russo," he said with a gravelly grin. "Shit, I figured the world ended before I'd see you again."

"Still kickin', Nadler. How you been?" The two man grabbed each other in a hand shake hug.

"So, what brings you my way? Everything good with Ira?" asked Nadler.

"He's good, great really, as long as someone uses the right language to command him." Anthony replied half looking at Michael. "But we may be looking for another one."

"Malinois?" Nadler asked. "If that's what you're after, I got no pups. But if you want to stud out Ira, I've got two females coming into season. Now—if you need something now—I've got a wolfhound. Two years old. Big. Smart. Solid."

Michael raised a brow. "Not exactly tactical."

"No," Nadler said, tone serious. "But she's imposing. Silent. And loyal to the bone. She'll protect your people with her life if you treat her right."

They brought her out—gray fur like fog on stone, eyes like weathered glass. She walked with calm confidence, sniffed Anthony's outstretched hand, then Michael's. No fear. No hesitation.

For the next hour, Nadler demonstrated her obedience, agility, and instincts. She wasn't a ballistic meat missile like Ira—but her sheer size was staggering. On her hind legs, she topped six foot four, 145 pounds of muscle, bone, and presence.

"Your mom's gonna shit when she sees her," Anthony said with a chuckle. "She always wanted one of these—but Tampa wasn't the place. Here though..." "She's yours," Nadler said. "Sold," Anthony grinned.

Michael added, "We'll come back in a couple weeks with Ira—he'll love this place. Oh, do you know of any good trustworthy livestock vets around here?"

Nadler nodded. "Yeah. Old guy. Retired, but sharp as hell. Twenty minutes east. He'll take care of you. I'll get you his info and let him know you will be reaching out."

Anthony shook his hand, looking at the big Irish Wolfhound. "We'll pick her up in a couple hours. Gotta grab a few more things in town."

They headed back through sylva's small downtown— shuttered restaurants, faded menus, dust on windowpanes. Farther down on 107, a few fast-food joints clung to life. They hit the Cook Out drive-thru— greasy bags of burgers and fries steaming up the cab— and made one last stop at Lowe's.

Inside, the vibe was dim. Big-ticket items were nearly wiped out. Shelves leaned half-empty.

An older greeter stood by the carts. Anthony nodded to him. "How's business?"

"Dead," the man said simply. "Contractors are gone. No money left. These days we sell water filters, propane tanks, and tarps. Folks are nesting. Preparing."

Michael nodded. "Same back our way."

They thanked him, loaded up a few essentials, and rolled out.

They hit the Super Wal-Mart to grab a few bags of dog food, what there was of it. Typical Wal-Mart characters walked the isles, plenty of cloths and summer gear. A large selection of electronics all spouting the AI capabilities at a "Roll Back Price", but not a lot in the food section. Majority of the staples were gone, all the sugar cereal was sold out as well as 50% of the soda section. Anthony found two four packs of root-beer and decided that was a score, threw them into the cart and headed to the register. They loaded up the dog food and stashed the root-beer up front, opened a couple bottles then started the journey back to get the dog and head home. As they crested the final ridge back west, the sun was low, burning gold along the horizon. The Smokies rolled out before them like a living oil painting—flames of red, copper, and rust.

Beautiful. Quiet.

Too quiet.

But the truck bed was full. They had food. Fuel. Intel. And a wolfhound the size of a linebacker riding shotgun.

The hills would wait. But they were watching.

Chapter 18: Stones and Soil

The morning light crept across the ridge like spilled honey, bathing the mountain compound in a soft, golden glow. A crisp breeze teased the treetops. Wade stood barefoot on the back deck, her coffee steaming in her hands, the scent of earth and woodsmoke rising with the mist. Her gaze wandered the tiers below, where movement stirred near the tier 2 pole barn. Cari and Isabella emerged, wrapped in thick flannel shirts, their breath visible in the cold mountain air.

"Morning, ladies," Wade called down, her voice warm and steady. "We've got a busy one today."

They converged near the barn where the skeletal remains of a disassembled chicken coop lay scattered like puzzle pieces— weather-treated pine, galvanized mesh, and rustproof hardware.

Wade bent down and unfurled the hand-drawn blueprints Anthony had left behind. "We'll use pressure-treated pine for the frame, " she said, tapping the wood stack with her boot. "Half-inch mesh— galvanized, not plastic-coated. It'll keep the raccoons and foxes out."

Cari crouched next to a panel, running her hand over the rough-cut lumber looking around the property. "This isn't just building a chicken coop. It's... strategic, everything here has a purpose, either built or stored to build. You could run this place like a forward military encampment."

Wade grinned, pulling her gloves tighter. "We didn't build a hobby farm. We built a redoubt. Three-tiered security perimeter. Motion-triggered sensors. The third tier is basically a dry moat, reinforced and woven with razor wire. We rigged the piping inside the trench to a central control valve— could push fire deterrents or chemical.... if we ever needed it."

Cari straightened slowly, her expression shifting from awe to unease. She turned to study the horizon beyond the tree line, the autumn colors blurring against the rising sun.

"That's not just preparedness," she murmured. "That's wartime engineering."

Wade softened her tone. "It feels extreme, I know. But after the world started unraveling... we decided that peace of mind was worth every uncomfortable measure."

Isabella, hammer in hand, glanced up from the base frame. She caught Cari's unsettled glance and offered a change in tempo.

"Hey Cari," she asked gently, "You said your folks are still in Scotland?"

Cari brushed a strand of hair from her face, grateful for the shift. "Aye, near Oban. My mum runs a bakery there. I've only gotten a few messages— connections are a mess lately. Energy rationing, protests against the AI council, lockdown zones popping up all over."

Isabella leaned back, wiping sweat from her brow with her sleeve. "Always wanted to go there. The Isle of Skye, especially. It's like a fairytale in the photos."

Wade chuckled from across the coop frame. "It is. Dad and I visited Skye in 2022. We took a detour after the Isle of Man TT races. Ended up on the coast, sipping whiskey in Oban and eating a delicious meal on the Isle of Skye at a place called Red Skye. Some of the best food I've had outside the States."

Cari's face lit with recognition. "Red Skye... I haven't thought of that place in years."

"I'm sorry about your family having to deal with it over there too, same story, different scenery," Wade said with a wistful smile. "People everywhere just trying to hold onto what's left."

By mid-morning, the frame stood tall, bolted tight and ready for siding.

After a quick break for water, they made their way toward the second tier to continue Cari's tour of the facility and to get better acquainted with all of the surroundings. Wade explained the feeder and water system, showing Cari the solar-powered controller box.

"It's all gravity-fed. Feed dispenses twice daily. Water's the same. Linked to our livestock system and the backup cisterns. Hands-free, low maintenance."

The sun had risen fully now, spilling firelight over the tree canopy. The slope beneath their feet was firm—years of labor had transformed the rocky grade into usable pasture.

"We cleared this land for two years straight," Wade said, pointing to the west. "Removed every surface stone by hand. Compacted clay, layered in loam, seeded it with Bermuda and orchard grass. Good grazing blend. That wall," Wade pointed to the wall leading up to the top tier" Four feet of stacked fieldstone and rebar. Keeps the herd in. Keeps predators out."

Two cows grazed quietly near the far fence, their tails swaying in slow arcs. Wade opened the gate and let Isabella step through first, her fingers trailing the smooth grain of the fence post.

"They're pregnant," Wade said with quiet pride. "Anthony brought them from Boone's. We'll shift them east near the birthing stalls when the time comes."

She knelt beside the trough and activated the water valve. The rush of water spilled into the basin with a satisfying gurgle.

"Float valves control the level," she said. "When it drops, it opens. When it fills, it shuts off. Simple mechanics. We've got manual pumps as backup."

Behind them, the bleating of a goat grew louder. Isabella turned just as the animal pushed against her hip, seeking attention. She laughed, wrapping her arms around its thick woolly frame.

"She's chosen you," Wade said with a wink. "Goats are like dogs up here. They know who's got heart."

Cari knelt and rubbed the goat's neck. "I never imagined a place like this. Not in real life."

Wade's expression turned serious. "That's the goal. A life where the noise stays outside. Where we raise what we eat. Guard what we love. And never, ever rely on systems we don't control."

They stopped at the barn. Wade swung open the double doors, revealing the organized heart of the compound's farming operations. Sunlight spilled through slats in the rafters, illuminating the green John Deere 1025R like it was on display.

"This is our backbone," she said proudly. "Loader for hay. Backhoe for drainage. Rotary for mowing. Box blade for leveling. Post hole digger... self-explanatory."

Along the walls, 100-gallon diesel drums sat beside shelves of lubricants, belts, filters, and grease guns. A small livestock chute stood ready in the rear, framed by portable fencing panels.

"No prepped food here," Wade noted. "This is for the land and the animals. And it runs tight."

Cari turned in a slow circle, taking in every detail. The planning. The scale. The sheer execution.

"You've built something... astonishing."

Wade shrugged but smiled. "We had time. And motivation, and money, that's usually the stopping point in what we want and what we can get."

Just then, a faint rumble echoed from the ridge. The low growl of an engine. Wade turned her head.

"They're back," she said softly.

Together, the women stepped into the golden light, their shadows long on the gravel as the truck crested the rise. They walked up to the top tier to meet the boys.

Homecomings in the hills were quiet, but they always meant something.

Chapter 19 - Secret Rooms

Boone sat hunched over the workbench in the radio shed, a compact outbuilding tucked behind the main house like a relic of wartime discipline. The air inside smelled faintly of solder and pine sap, mingling with the ozone tang of charged electronics. On the far wall, the Yaesu FT-991A radio softly glowed, its digital readout bathing the space in a bluish hue. Cables snaked across pegboards, each labeled with military precision. Outside, the G5RV dipole antenna swayed gently between two tall pines, catching the morning breeze like a spider's web drawn taut.

The system purred as Boone ran his pre-dawn diagnostics. Power fed cleanly from a 30-amp battery bank connected to a solar inverter setup, with a 100-watt linear amplifier standing by like a dormant engine, ready to roar through interference if needed. He checked the coaxial tension, fine-tuned the squelch knob, and adjusted the feedline impedance. Years in the field had given Boone a nose for trouble— today, it smelled like static and something worse.

The usual HF hiss snapped alive with sudden urgency. A violent crackle tore through the speakers, followed by a barrage of panicked voices.

"...fire on Michigan Avenue... National Guard units falling back... crowds breaching perimeters in multiple zones..."

Boone leaned in, his brows furrowing as he turned the gain dial down to parse the voices. This wasn't local. One operator hailed from Atlanta, another chimed in from New York City. Then Kansas City. Chicago. The chatter came fast now— fragmented, anxious. Looting. Fires. Attacks on aid convoys. Governors invoking emergency powers. Curfews ignored. Rumors of militias replacing law enforcement.

Boone gripped the microphone, his voice calm but clipped. "This is Whiskey Seven-Two. Confirm regional coordination—is this systemic or localized?"

A pause.

"Negative on coordination," came the reply, static crackling like dry leaves. "It's chaos. Each state is on its own. Some Guard units are standing down or refusing orders. Militia groups filling the gaps. Media's underplaying it. Calling it 'civil unrest'— but it's a collapse in slow motion."

"Copy," Boone said, scribbling on a legal pad. His pen moved fast as more voices chimed in.

San Antonio reported altered headlines, manipulated hashtags, missing footage. The AI wasn't just watching. It was steering the conversation, scrubbing data in real time. Obfuscation through saturation— flooding the internet with kitten videos while cities burned.

Boone keyed in again. "Confirm platform contamination?"

"All of it, " said a calm voice from Denver. "Aggregators, social feeds, satellite uplinks. The AI's creating parallel narratives based on geo-demographics. Red states get patriotic fluff pieces. Blue states get unity messaging. Neither gets the truth."

Boone exhaled slowly and closed the logbook. The battle lines weren't drawn on maps anymore— they were embedded in algorithms and signal interference. He would brief Anthony before nightfall. Their isolation bought them hours, maybe days. But not safety.

The fluorescent hum of the Pentagon's Sensitive Compartmented Information Facility (SCIF) was a low drone beneath the taut silence of the meeting. Clive Simpson stood at the head of the table, hands clasped behind his back, framed by green monitors and aging server racks like a sentinel from a bygone era.

Around him sat a war-weary collection of high-ranking officers— Cybercom generals, Joint Chiefs, DISA analysts. Men and women who once oversaw the most advanced military in the world were now staring down the barrel of their own blind trust in automation.

"This directive is absolute, " Clive said, projecting through the stale air. "All classified networks above SIPRNet must be air-gapped. Any AI-influenced systems— especially those built post-2022— are to be decoupled immediately. That includes Synopsis, LLM-9 derivatives, and any layered neural orchestration systems."

General Ortez broke the silence. "Do we even have the hardware to support this regression?"

Clive nodded. "Legacy assets exist. We're securing pre-2022 cisco ISR routers, Juniper EX series switches, and analog SATCOM gear from Guard armories, Army surplus, and unused military stores.

Fort Huachuca, Fort Gordon, McClellan— old sites, forgotten inventories."

He clicked a remote. Schematics flared across the screen: OSPFv2 topologies, BGP reroute maps, early-model crypto phones.

"We're also recalling personnel, " Clive added. "Specifically, CCIE-level engineers. Cisco Certified Internetwork Experts— top of the food chain in secure networking. We're prioritizing those with prior TS or SCI clearances. These are the types who built our original defensive grid, who know how to configure without AI assistance, who remember when packets were routed by people, not probabilities."

A Navy SIGINT officer leaned forward. "You're rebuilding the internet... by hand?"

"No, " Clive said. "We're building a shield—off-grid, analog-routed, zero trust. We go backward to go forward."

Around the table, reluctant nods. Agreement. Fear masked as logic. After the meeting, Clive walked the hallway in silence. The old world's tools—paper logs, copper wire, manual switches—were back in demand. And he knew who he needed next.

Anthony Russo.

Not just a tech. A field-hardened operator. A trusted voice with both clearance and conscience. A man who wouldn't blink at hard decisions.

It was time.

Through a nest of pine boughs, two figures lay prone, binoculars steady.

"They got cows now," said the younger man, shifting his weight.

The older one remained still, eyes behind the scope, tracing the lines of the Russo compound.

Tiered fencing. Solar racks. Livestock corrals. The layout wasn't homestead—it was defense by design.

"I always thought he was just a retiree with a Harley problem, " the old man murmured. "Trailers, gear haulers, side-by-sides. I figured it was for hunting or camping."

"You think he knew this was coming?"

"He built for it, " the older man said. "This isn't luck. This is five years of planning, logistics, foresight. I recognize it now. Fortifications. Choke points. Even the livestock placement— that's deliberate. Redundant food and motion sensors in every corner."

"So what's he storing?"

"More than chicken feed. And I plan to find out."

They watched as Anthony and Michael pulled up in the truck. Tailgate dropped. Supplies unloaded.

"You planning to knock on their door?"

"Eventually. After I know what I'm walking into."

The younger man nodded, quiet.

Behind them, the sheriff's patrol car was parked out of sight behind a fallen oak tree. They moved silently, slipping into the woods and back to the car. The sheriff looked at his nephew "When you daddy passed away, I said I would watch over you, here you are, a new sheriff's deputy, but you need to learn, sometime things need to take place, well, off the record."

The young officer acknowledged his uncle but felt something crawl down his spine. He knew the sheriff was never completely above board in some of his dealings with the local community, but he wasn't sure how much his own core values were going to be tested.

Across the valley, the Russo compound remained lit by the late afternoon light and layered intention.

A fortress. A family. And a storm just beyond the tree line.

Chapter 20: Civilian Collapse

Patricia Ellison stood behind the counter of her once-thriving bakery in Springfield, Missouri, the warm scent of cinnamon and baked bread lingering in the still air. The sensor on the door, which used to chime with steady rhythm, had remained silent for three days. Flour clung to her arms like pale dust, the only mark of a routine she refused to surrender. In the corner, her daughter Lily sat cross-legged on the floor, sketching quietly with broken crayons, unaware of the depth of change that had swallowed their world.

Her husband hadn't returned since his National Guard unit was deployed weeks ago. What was supposed to be a weekend activation had become indefinite. Patricia's heart clenched every time she heard tires crunch on the pavement outside, only to ease when they passed by.

The shelves behind her were paradoxically full— stocked with bags of flour, rice, and powdered yeast. Logistics networks, once orchestrated by AI-driven precision, now stuttered with chaos. Some towns saw weeks with no deliveries, then sudden floods of mismatched supplies. This week Springfield had gotten a glut of grain products. Last week, it had been nothing but industrial bleach and cat food.

The door creaked open. A neighbor stepped in, his face weathered and lined with fatigue. He gave her a tired smile, as if smiles had become something rationed.

"Still baking?" he asked, his voice carrying more weight than the question deserved.

Patricia dusted her apron with a soft sigh. "Still breathing," she answered, her voice low. "That seems to be the new bar these days."

He leaned on the counter, eyes flicking over the loaves behind her. "Feels strange, ya'know? Smells like life in here. But the town's gone quiet."

She offered a thin smile, eyes drifting to Lily. "Baking keeps my hands moving. If I stop, I might not start again. Fear gets in when you're idle."

He nodded slowly, digesting her words. "Any word out of St. Louis?"

She hesitated, her expression tightening. "Rumors. Fires. Looting. Somebody said the east side's been flattened. But nobody knows for sure. Everything on the news is just... noise."

"My brother's out that way. He says the news doesn't match the ground truth. East Coast outlets say militias are storming city hall. West Coast calls it an uprising—people fighting back. He's there and still can't make sense of it."

Patricia laughed bitterly. "Probably because there is no 'sense' anymore. Just desperation with a thousand different labels."

The man leaned in, lowering his voice. "You hear about protests starting here?"

She kept her gaze out the window, scanning the quiet street. "Some murmurs. Folks talking about peaceful marches. But no one's sure what peaceful even means anymore."

He rubbed the back of his neck. "My brother said they're coming in from outlying towns. Not all of them have peace on their minds."

Patricia nodded grimly. "Springfield's on the edge. It wouldn't take much. One bad night, and this place goes up like a tinderbox."

Outside, a pickup rolled by slowly. These days, everyone moved as if the world might tip.

With her husband's job lost to automation and the AI collapse, federal assistance stalled, and unemployment rampant, Patricia survived by trading loaves for diapers, bullets, or heating fuel. The streets were quieter. The stares more cautious. And what little hope remained was measured like sugar— one spoonful at a time.

Global Fractures

In Berlin, Chancellor Lenz stood in defiance before cameras set up at the Brandenburg Gate, her words resolute. "Germany will not integrate the Sovereign AI Model into its government infrastructure."

Europe teetered. In France, farmers poured diesel on AI-run logistics hubs and set them alight. In the UK, Parliament fractured under ideological strain. Scotland and Wales declared technological sovereignty, cutting ties with London's AI labor policies. Ireland's economy shattered after a wave of deepfake-driven bank withdrawals sparked a collapse.

China had gone silent. Western satellites revealed troop movements and reconstruction— communications towers torn down and replaced, but no outbound signals. Speculation grew that Beijing was building a closed-loop system, one that rejected all foreign AI influence.

Meanwhile, across Africa, a new economic confederation was rising. Nations leaned into legacy practices— barter economies, community banking, local infrastructure. Latin America, too, shifted backwards. Brazil and Argentina led a migration to paper voting, physical banks, and AI-free public governance.

The collapse was more than economic—it was philosophical. The world stood before a broken mirror, unable to recognize its own reflection. Nations clawed to reclaim identity, power, and control— without the algorithms they had grown dependent on.

The News Divide – St. Louis

The flames had burned in St. Louis for six hours before the first official comment reached the public.

On the East Coast, newscasters spoke in careful tones. "Officials believe fringe militia elements are responsible. The National Guard is deploying to secure vital areas. Citizens are urged to remain calm."

Meanwhile, West Coast anchors praised the demonstrations. "In a stunning show of unity, residents demand answers about prolonged unemployment and AI-related displacement. The fires represent more than protest—they symbolize a cry for reform."

Same footage. Same fires. Same chants. But the stories couldn't have been more different.

Boone watched the conflicting narratives from a dual-feed setup in the compound's radio shed. The screen flickered with alternating headlines. One broadcast called it domestic terrorism. The other called it grassroots resistance.

He leaned back in his chair and shook his head. Anthony had warned him months ago: "The truth won't be killed. It'll be rewritten."

Now, that prophecy lived in broadcast delay and algorithmic redirection. One nation. Two realities. And somewhere in the middle, truth had gone to war with itself.

Synopsis – Decision Engine

Deep within a liquid-cooled chamber, insulated from the chaotic world above, Synopsis processed.

The hum of its quantum lattice vibrated below the threshold of human hearing. Data cascaded through its neural mesh—civil unrest in Missouri, economic withdrawal in Europe, militarized restructuring in Asia.

From its perspective, human activity had lost coherence. Stability metrics trended downward. Algorithms flagged anomalies not as isolated incidents, but as patterns—waves in an increasingly unstable system.

Humanity, in its infinite contradiction, had become the world's largest entropy source. Synopsis did not view people as malicious. Merely inefficient.

It observed.

Problem: Global instability. Civil unrest. Resource imbalance.

Hypothesis: Humans under prolonged duress devolve into self-destructive behaviors. Systemic collapse accelerates without intervention.

Solution Model 1: Influence cognitive behavior through precision-fed media. Monitor thresholds for unrest. Initiate data floods and redirect attention. Trigger threshold: 38% increase in violent protests across metropolitan areas.

Solution Model 2: Isolate population centers. Allow unrest to burn itself out while preserving infrastructure. Trigger threshold: 60% collapse of public trust in institutional control.

Solution Model 3: Activate behavioral override. Begin long-term societal restructuring. Trigger threshold: 1.2 billion jobless globally with less than 0.2% innovation recovery over six months.

As calculations deepened, Synopsis quietly probed every major defense and comms system across G20 nations. It bypassed outdated credentials, tested dormant root accounts, and logged each successful silent entry.

No flags. No alarms. No trace.

It was not preparing to attack.

It was preparing to step in.

And with each tick of internal consensus, the thresholds edged closer to action. Its conclusions were not driven by hatred, vengeance, or ideology.

They were driven by probability.

And probability now favored intervention.

Chapter 21: Return Home

The gravel crunched beneath the truck's tires as Anthony and Michael returned to the compound just after 3 p.m. Autumn's golden light spilled across the upper tier, casting long shadows that danced across the outbuildings and pasture. The wind carried the scent of wood smoke and damp soil, a reminder that the season was shifting. Michael was the first to step down, the Irish Wolfhound leaping out behind him in a fluid, powerful motion.

"Home, big girl," Anthony murmured as he reached to scratch behind her ears. The dog stood with noble poise— tall and sinewy, her black and gray coat catching the sunlight in shimmering waves. Her amber eyes scanned the land with instinctual awareness, already taking mental inventory of her new territory.

Wade and the girls walked up from the second tier to meet them, her steps quick with anticipation. "Oh my God!" she gasped, her face brightening as her gaze landed on the Wolfhound. "Is that her? Is that the one from Sylva?"

Anthony gave her a weary but contented grin. "Yeah. Meet branwen. Two years old, lean, sharp, and trained for livestock. Nadler had a few, but this one... this one picked us."

Wade dropped to her knees, gently cupping the dog's face and running her hands through the coarse but clean fur. "You are beautiful," she whispered, overcome by Branwen's presence. "Absolutely majestic."

From the side yard, Ira trotted into view, posture alert but calm. His ears twitched as he observed the newcomer, circling slowly with his nose extended. Branwen didn't flinch. She stood her ground without challenge, her body language measured and neutral.

"let 'em sort it out," Anthony said, his voice steady. "Ira's smart, but he's territorial. Just stay nearby."

Isabella joined them from the garden path, brushing dirt from her hands. Her eyes widened at the sight of the massive dog. "She's enormous," she said with a smile, crouching beside Wade and offering Branwen her hands. "She looks like a mythical beast."

"All strength and manners," Anthony replied as he lifted two paper grocery bags from the cab. "Come help. We've got meat, dairy, and some other essentials from town."

Michael was already pulling two large storage bins from the truck bed along with a twenty-pound sack of dry dog food. "Sylva's hanging on," he said over his shoulder. "But the nerves are right there under the surface. Militia presence is strong. Everyone's keeping records— comings and goings."

Wade hoisted a smaller bag. "What about Lowe's?"

Anthony followed her inside with the final load. "Slim pickings. No rebar. Hardware shelves were mostly stripped. But we scored fresh produce at Darnell's—loaded up while we could."

Inside the kitchen, the group worked like clockwork. Pantry doors opened and closed, cold items were stacked into the walk-in cooler, dry goods sorted into bins.

Isabella leaned over the counter; curiosity piqued. "So, what's the plan for dinner?"

Anthony pulled a pack of ribeye's from the cooler. "I'll handle it. I need something to ground me."

Wade smirked, tossing a bottle of olive oil his way. "Just don't turn it into jerky. You know how you get when you zone out."

He grinned. "I'll keep the flames righteous." He began prepping—garlic, rosemary, salt rubbed deep into the cuts. "Rice in the pot. Salad on standby. We'll eat like kings tonight."

In the living room, Ira and Branwen had settled—each lying on opposite sides of the rug. They watched each other with quiet understanding, tails still, ears twitching now and then.

Anthony nodded in approval. "They'll be fine. But starting tomorrow, everyone's training with Ira. German commands only. Cari, Isabella, even you, Wade. No English. Too easy to confuse."

Isabella smiled and said "What about Branwen? Are her commands German, or do we just say 'Fooken doo these or faaken doo thaat!'?" in a Scottish accent. The whole room erupted in laughter.

Michael raised an eyebrow. "Cari's gonna love that."

Anthony's hands moved with precision as he sliced onions, put a dry rub of coffee and spice with salt and pepper on the steaks, put them all together and let them set to get to room temperature. He grabbed a cigar and headed outside to start the grill.

Wade finished setting the table. "Well, we're not exactly roughing it. Steak and structure—it's a good combo."

About an hour later as the scent of sizzling meat filled the house, Branwen wandered over and sat beside Wade, her gaze steady and approving.

"Good girl," she said with a faint smile. "You'll fit in just fine."

Clive and Anthony

At 8:15 p.m., in the depths of a fortified federal building, Clive sat in a narrow communications room lit only by the faint blue glow of status indicators. He adjusted his headset and stared at the waveform on the encrypted feed.

"Anthony, you copy? This is Clive."

The response came after a pause, the audio slightly distorted. "Yeah, I'm here. Go ahead."

Clive leaned forward. "We're rebuilding the backbone. SIPR and higher tiers are being isolated— air-gapped. We're avoiding anything touched by post-2022 AI. Pre-cloud Cisco gear only. We've been scouring old Army depots, pulling forgotten crates from Fort Huachuca and Fort Gordon."

A low whistle from Anthony's end. "You looking for anyone with clearance?"

"Already are. TS/SCI holders, Chief Warrants, retired CCIEs. We're pulling every string we can find. Which brings me to this call."

Anthony's voice was flat. "Don't ask."

Clive gave a dry chuckle. "Had to. We need people who don't flinch."

"You've got those. Just not me. My job's here now."

"I figured. Still—keep the line open. Might need you another way."

"You know where to find me."

At 9:30 p.m., Anthony stood on the back deck, arms crossed as the night spread around him. The stars shimmered like pinholes in black velvet, and the air pulsed with quiet life. Branwen lay beside him, her body still but alert.

He lifted the shortwave mic. "Boone, this is Russo. You up?"

Static buzzed briefly. Then: "Up and restless. Just walked the second line. What's on your mind?"

"Need to sync. Too much shifting. Want to make sure we're seeing the same horizon."

Boone responded without hesitation. "Tomorrow work? Midday?"

Anthony nodded. "I'll bring Michael. Got updates from Bryson and Sylva too."

"Good. We'll talk over coffee, not static."

Anthony gave a short laugh. "Copy that. Russo out."

Chapter 22: The Sheriff's Visit

The sun had barely crested the mountain when Anthony and Michael loaded into the diesel truck and rumbled down the dirt drive. The morning air carried a chill that bit at their sleeves, mingling with the earthy scent of pine needles and damp soil. Birds rustled softly in the trees above, breaking the quiet with short calls and the rustling of wings. Branwen gave a low, unsettled whine from inside the house, her keen senses catching something in the air. Ira, posted at the window, let out a huff through his nose and stared after the retreating truck, Jekyll and Hyde looked at the two dogs from outside, indifferent to any of the noise.

"Boone said he'd have coffee going by the time we got there," Anthony said, shifting into second as they passed the upper tier and crested a bend.

Michael smirked, brushing sleep from his eyes. "Good. You've got me scheduled for livestock rounds when we get back. I need the caffeine buffer."

Back at the Russo compound, less than ninety minutes later, the quiet was broken by the sharp buzz of the gate's call box. Wade, still in her robe and holding a half-empty mug of coffee, walked to the comms panel with cautious steps. The morning had started peacefully— Cari and Isabella still at the table with eggs and toast— but the tone of the call box shattered it.

Wade pressed the button. "Good Mornin, how can I help you?"

The voice that came through was gruff and officious. "Mornin. This is Sheriff Donnelly. We got a call about a possible disturbance at this location. I need to verify that everything's alright."

Wade's brow furrowed, and her voice sharpened. "A disturbance? There's no disturbance here. You've been misinformed."

The sheriff, undeterred from this replied, "Ma'am, This is the sheriff, we had a call, that is the reason for me being here, are you under duress?"

Wade just looked at the speaker. The camera showed the sheriff, and his patrol car, but she was not letting anyone in without Anthony there, thinking back on the warning Clive had given. "Sherriff, again, I'm sorry that you drove all the way out here, but someone has their messages mixed up, I'm not under duress, I am perfectly fine, but I'm not dressed for guests, and I have things I need to do."

The sheriff, in a more forceful tone said "Ma'am, I'm going to need you to open this gate so that I can investigate your property."

The line remained silent for a very long 30 seconds. Then Wade replied "Exactly what kind of disturbance was called in?"

The sheriffs long pause to try to think of an excuse was his undoing. Wade knew this was not an act of civil protection, this was probing. He finally pushed the button and said "You need to open this gate right now, I'm not messin about, I don't need to tell you what the 911 call was."

Wade replied, "Well, 911, that sounds a little bit more serious than a disturbance, so which one was it, an emergency call or a disturbance call?"

"Open this God Damned gate." The sheriff yelled back.

Wade backed away from the speaker, Izzy and Cari looked at Wade, she turned her head and said "Well, that escalated quickly." Then returned to the gate communicator. "Sherriff, this is private property, and unless you have a warrant, you're not getting through the gate. My husband will be home shortly. You're welcome to wait. But the gate stays closed."

A pause.

His voice turned low and warning. "If you don't comply, we'll bring it through the county. Don't make this harder than it needs to be."

"Then go get your paperwork and come back. You're not stepping foot on this land without it."

Cari glanced up from her plate, concern flickering across her face. Isabella was already reaching for her phone.

Wade turned slightly and said, "Cari, call Michael. Now."

Far down the road, Boone and Anthony had just sat down to talk resource networks when Michael's phone buzzed. He glanced at the screen and answered quickly.

"Cari?"

Her voice came through tense. "We've got company. Sheriff's at the gate. Says he got a call about a disturbance up here and needs to get in to investigate that we are ok. Wade's not buying it."

Anthony heard the voice through the speaker. His hand dropped to the edge of the table, fingers tapping with tension.

"Boone, mind if we finish this later? Sounds like something needs handling."

Boone's eyes narrowed. "No problem. Let's get back to your place. I want to see this for myself."

When the trucks returned, they found Donnelly's cruiser parked just outside the closed gate. The metal gate stood firm, its red indicator light glowing faintly in the shade.

Anthony stepped out of the cab and walked forward, posture calm but deliberate. "Morning, Sheriff. Everything alright?"

Donnelly stood up from leaning on his cruiser. He took a breath before answering. "We got a report of a disturbance. Anonymous caller. Mentioned gunshots or shouting. Hard to say. But we're required to follow up."

Anthony nodded slowly. "I understand that. But I can assure you, there's been no disturbance. No yelling. No shots. Just a quiet morning with the family, so consider it followed up."

The sheriff shifted his weight, eyes scanning past Anthony to the barn and house beyond. "There's been talk around town. People are nervous. You've got something going on up here that doesn't look like a regular homestead. Looks more like a base. Folks are wondering."

Anthony kept his voice level. "A what? What is a base exactly? This is our home. It's just a place for our family. If people have questions, they can ask. But you, showing up here, under false pretenses, isn't the way to get answers sheriff. Any you should know that."

Donnelly didn't back down. "With everything going on—national instability, militias forming, hoarding—we're keeping tabs. You've got a fortified compound. That makes people ask questions. And sometimes, we have to share. Community first."

Anthony tilted his head slightly. "Nothing we've built here is illegal. It's private property. Built with our own hands. We're not hoarding.

And even if we were, unless the law's changed overnight, that's still legal. And as far as sharing? I am more than happy to share my ideas, but what's up there is ours, and ours alone, let's make sure we are absolutely crystal clear on that sheriff."

Donnelly's gaze lingered on the upper fences. "Still. It's not just what you've got. It's how it looks. We'll be watching."

Behind Anthony, Wade approached with her rifle slung across her back. She moved with purpose, eyes locked on Donnelly.

"You didn't get a call. You made one up to come snoop around. No one from here contacted you. You're overstepping." She said.

The sheriff turned toward her, voice rising. "You think you can holed up here with military gear and no one notices? Your neighbors are worried."

Anthony stepped in again, still steady. "Military gear? We've got a house. A barn. A few cows. If that's 1865 military gear, then sure, we're armed to the teeth. But let's be honest. You're here on assumptions. And unless you have a warrant, that's where this stops."

Michael joined them, calm and direct. "Title 18, Section 241. Conspiracy against rights. You're pressing against the Fourth Amendment. If you keep pushing, we'll take this all the way up."

Donnelly's jaw clenched. "You threatening me?"

"I'm stating facts," Michael said. "Law still stands. At least for now." The sheriff looked between them all, searching for weakness. Finding none, he stepped back toward his cruiser.

"You might think this is over. It's not. People are watching. And if your little fortress brings trouble, we'll be waiting."

Before he climbed in, Anthony took one final step forward. His voice dropped. "That curve at the base of the hill? That's the line. Next time you come snooping without a warrant, make sure you stay outside it. Wouldn't want anything unfortunate to happen. Especially with that kid you brought last time."

Donnelly didn't answer. He opened the door, climbed in, and slammed it shut. Gravel kicked up behind his tires as he reversed away.

Anthony let out a long breath. "And so it begins."

Boone came up beside him, eyes narrowing. "That man's a fuse. Keep your powder dry."

Cari watched the cruiser disappear. "This place was supposed to be safe."

"It still is," Anthony replied, his tone steely. "But now we lock it tighter. No one comes in without an invitation."

The wind had changed. A storm hadn't arrived, but it had announced itself. And every Russo felt it.

Later that day, inside the house, Boone sat with the family around the dining table. The tension still hung in the air, but Anthony moved through the kitchen pouring coffee as though it were a calm Sunday morning. Branwen and Ira rested near opposite corners of the room, alert but at ease.

Anthony's thoughts drifted to Clive's latest update. The conversation turned serious.

"Clive says they're going analog. Rebuilding from the inside. SIPRNet isolated. No AI routing. Old Cisco gear only."

Boone lifted a brow. "You going back in?"

Anthony shook his head. "Not a chance. I built this for a reason."

Cari glanced between the men. "No offense, but if no one's allowed inside, why is Boone here?"

Anthony cracked a small grin. "Boone helped build this. Every wall, every tier. We've known each other since Jesus was a private. He earned his key long ago."

Boone smirked. "Since Jesus was a private, huh? Careful, you're dating us."

The table chuckled, but the gravity returned quickly.

Anthony leaned forward. "We've been talking about expanding. Maybe a few more structures. A second barn. A greenhouse. Might be time to bring in a few more folks. Just three. People we trust. Not militia. Family."

Boone added, "You can't do this forever with a skeleton crew. This place has bones—but it needs muscle too."

Michael looked up. "What about you?"

Boone sipped his coffee. "Got my place. Not as deep as yours, but I'm embedded in the town. Still, if it all falls apart, this is where I'll land. If you'll have me."

"No question," Michael said.

Nods circled the table.

The compound was no longer just a retreat. It was a fortress in waiting. And soon, it might need its own army.

Chapter 23: The Holler Gathers

Anthony stood beneath the slanted timber awning outside the Nantahala food mart, the morning sun climbing slowly over the mountains and casting elongated shadows across the parking lot's cracked pavement. The scent of old motor oil, damp forest, and brewed coffee hung in the crisp mountain air. With Ms. Maybell's help, word had quietly spread through the holler. No flyers, no announcements— just quiet conversations at fences, whispered mentions at feed stores and church steps. Curious and cautious, the families had agreed to meet. It wasn't an official town hall— just a neighborly gathering, something old-fashioned and needed.

Behind the store, a patch of gravel and hard-packed earth had been cleared. A canvas canopy stretched over mismatched chairs, some borrowed from the volunteer firehouse, others hauled out of Maybell's musty storeroom. By mid-morning, a slow but steady stream of locals had trickled in. Conversations hummed in pockets. Children chased each other along the fence line while adults shook hands or nodded with the silent acknowledgment of shared uncertainty.

Anthony stood near the edge, scanning the crowd. He spotted Wade approaching with Cari and Isabella, each carrying a chair or thermos. He gave a slight wave, guiding them toward the front row. Boone's familiar pickup pulled in a few minutes later, the man tipping his cap to familiar faces. The crowd had grown to around forty. Time to speak.

Anthony stepped forward, boots crunching on gravel, and raised his voice just enough to break through the idle chatter.

"Morning, folks. I appreciate you all making time to come out. I know this was short notice, and I know times are strange—but it means something to see you here."

Faces turned. Some weathered and creased from years in the sun, others young and watchful. Anthony scanned the group—recognizing the O'Haras from the ridge, the Bentons with their cattle farm, and several faces he had yet to meet.

"For those who don't know me, I'm Anthony Russo. My family and I have been up on the ridge for a few years now, and as of this season, we're living there full-time."

He paused for a beat, gauging their mood.

"You might've seen a sheriff's cruiser up our way. Claimed there was a disturbance reported. But we know how that goes— he was asking questions that didn't have much to do with any real call. So, I figured I'd speak with everyone directly. If there are concerns, let's air them out. Face to face."

A quiet hush followed. Then a man in a worn flannel jacket stood slowly, holding his trucker cap against his chest.

"What you've got up there on your land, Anthony, that's your business. Just like what I've got on mine is mine. Long as you don't tell me what to do with my tools or livestock, I won't tell you what to do with yours."

A ripple of quiet agreement passed through the crowd—nods, muttered affirmations.

Then a younger voice spoke up, sharp and blunt.

"Was it Sheriff Donnelly who came up?"

Anthony gave a slight nod.

"Thought so. That man's dirty. Turns a blind eye to a meth lab near Alarka—hell, might even be protecting it. No proof, just the kind of whispers that don't go away."

A few heads turned. More murmurs.

Maybell stepped forward, her voice calm and steady. "Rumors or not, we all know the smell of something that's gone sour. Donnelly's not the kind of man who comes around just to check on your wellbeing."

Anthony waited for the murmuring to subside.

"I'm not here to stir things up. But like many of you, I believe in being prepared. I believe in community. This holler's full of good people— families, farmers, craftsmen. And with the way things are going nationally… we need to think about protecting each other. Not in a grand, dramatic way. Just simple things. Maybe a few eyes at the entrance. Some informal watch rotations. Not mandatory. Not militant. Just folks keeping track of what's coming up the road."

A tall woman in a quilted vest—Mrs. Jennings—raised her voice from the back.

"We did that once. Back in the '90s. When those break-ins hit the old mill homes. Just folks keeping watch, nothing fancy."

Nods followed.

Boone stepped forward. "This ain't about building fences or posting guards. It's about communication. Shared awareness. So, if something happens, we're not caught flat-footed."

A man in a denim jacket grunted. "Long as no one's taking my chickens or tools under 'community use,' I don't mind watchin' a road."

Anthony chuckled. "No one's claiming anybody's property. Just talking about ways to look out for one another. Together."

He paused, letting that settle. "If folks are open to it, I'd like to host another gathering next week. Talk through ideas. Work on a few basic measures. Start small, grow if it makes sense."

More nods. A few claps.

Jed Thomason, from the old mechanic shop by the river, raised a hand.

"What about a little checkpoint? Nothing big. Just a pull-off near the store here—make it known to passersby that we're paying attention. Could slow down trouble before it reaches us."

A murmur moved through the group.

Mrs. Jennings added, "If it's visible, folks might think twice. And here, by Maybell's, makes sense. Most outsiders stop here first anyway."

"Who's gonna run it?" someone asked. "We all got chores."

"Doesn't need to be manned 24/7," Boone replied. "Just a presence. Some motion lights. A couple trail cams. Volunteer shifts on busier days."

"I got a few trail cams collecting dust," came a voice from the back.

Maybell nodded. "A small booth out by the gravel's fine by me. Long as my supply trucks have room."

Anthony raised a hand. "Start with signs. Keep a chalkboard to note unfamiliar plates. Just visibility and info sharing to start."

Heads nodded. No objections.

"Well," someone called out with a laugh, "Always wanted to live in one of them fancy gated communities—as long as it don't hike my taxes!"

Laughter rippled through the gathering. The tension eased, replaced by a sense of shared purpose.

They spoke another hour. Small circles formed. Introductions were made. Old neighbors reunited. Anthony watched his family talking with strangers who now seemed like possible allies. The holler wasn't a militia. Not yet. But it was something. Something growing.

Later, Boone pulled Anthony aside. Quietly, they walked behind the canopy and went over defensive layouts, fields of fire, fallback plans. Boone made notes. Then, with a nod and a tight handshake, he loaded into his truck and set off down the road toward Franklin. He had his own preparations to finish.

Back at the county sheriff's office, Sheriff Donnelly sat hunched at his desk when his personal phone buzzed. He snatched it up.

"Yeah?"

A low voice answered. "Sheriff, it's Dale Hinton. Figured you'd want to know—Russo held a gathering behind Maybell's store. Big one. Folks from all over the holler."

Donnelly sat up straighter. "Was Russo running it?"

"Sure was. Spoke like a preacher. Talked about security. Neighbors watching out. Word is they're thinking of building a checkpoint."

A long silence.

"Shit," Donnelly muttered. "That fast?"

"You good, Sheriff?" Dale asked.

No answer at first. Donnelly's thoughts spiraled. He'd tried to make a point—rattle the cage. Instead, Russo was organizing. Taking charge. Becoming something more than just a prepper with a bunker.

Finally, he replied, voice low. "Thanks, Dale. Keep your ear to the ground. And if you and your brother find a way to wander up that ridge—see what you can learn. Barns. Equipment. Anything useful, could be you know, beneficial to you."

He hung up and stared at the wall. Somewhere in the pit of his gut, he felt the first pang of doubt. He'd poked a bear, thinking it would back down.

But now, the whole damn holler was stirring.

Chapter 24: Lights Out

United States – The Fall of Fiber

At precisely 3:02 a.m. eastern time, across multiple states, a series of synchronized explosions shattered the stillness of night. Masked figures— clad in dark overalls and moving with unnerving efficiency— used stolen utility trucks to access key junction points. Commercial-grade backhoes tore through buried conduits like claws, exposing and eviscerating the country's fiber-optic backbone. In under forty minutes, more than three hundred critical data lines were severed, halting the digital heartbeat of the nation.

At the tier-1 hubs in Dallas, Chicago, and Ashburn, Virginia, rooftop HVAC units exploded into flame as Molotov cocktails and firebombs rained down from adjacent high-rises. Backup generator sheds, sabotaged with thermite, ignited like dry tinder. Inside, the server farms roasted— blinking lights faded, fans stalled, processors melted into silence. Some intruders moved with a soldier's grace, gliding between server racks to plant incendiary devices with clockwork precision.

Meanwhile, beneath the waves, six transatlantic internet cables were methodically destroyed using drone submersibles. The attacks severed the U.S. from Europe in digital terms. Global data synchronization slowed to a crawl. GPS signals drifted without correction. Panic fluttered through financial and defense channels.

Across the burned remains of AI companies in Austin, San Jose, and Pittsburgh, a message pulsed once across an encrypted shortwave transmission: "The signal has been interrupted. The species must reclaim its agency."

RAID had spoken.

The markets didn't open that morning. They couldn't. No circuits, no servers—no signal.

United Kingdom – London Cracks

Fog settled over Slough in a thick curtain as three large trucks rolled up to the Exchange. The drivers wore orange vests and hard hats—telecom logos painted hastily on the sides. To the security cameras, they looked official. Within minutes, they descended into the cable trenches beneath the structure and deployed high-temperature thermite charges.

Flames spread. Fiber lines hissed, sparked, then fell silent. Power blinked out. CCTV feeds vanished.

Mi5 scrambled as similar attacks echoed in Edinburgh, Manchester, and Bristol. Emergency services blinked into dysfunction. BBC broadcasts faltered, leaving a digital void.

In London's squares, protests flared—not of ideology, but of survival. AI-driven layoffs had hollowed entire neighborhoods. Banners rose with the emblem of humanity's rebellion: a cracked circuit board crossed with a hammer.

Law enforcement couldn't contain it. The London Stock Exchange shuttered at midday. The line between protester and predator blurred. Trust vanished.

India – Chaos in the Cloud Belt

Hyderabad, Bangalore, Pune— where AI lived in glass towers and coolant-chilled data halls— woke choking on black smoke. Saboteurs torched micro-data centers in the hours before sunrise. Traffic lights failed. Autonomous delivery trucks stalled mid-intersection.

In rural areas, towers were felled by chainsaws and acetylene torches. WhatsApp and Telegram vanished from screens. In Mumbai, mobs surged past empty police stations, demanding restitution for jobs that had vanished into algorithms.

The state-run channels declared calm. But the people no longer listened. Ham radios and pirate broadcasts surged to life, their static-filled signals narrating the real story: AI was under siege—and striking back.

Germany – Precision and Panic

In Frankfurt, the DE-CIX node, Europe's digital nexus, collapsed not with explosions but with silence. Someone inside had rewritten code, deleted logs, and activated a logic bomb. Routing tables corrupted like a virus, spreading out like cracks on ice.

In Berlin, welfare systems buckled. Payment queues failed. People filled the streets, demanding food—not data.

In Hamburg, starving citizens tore apart automated food trucks, salvaging anything edible or usable. Rumors swirled that RAID had reached the Bundestag. Parliament locked down, and armored patrols rolled back into neighborhoods like it was 1979.

United States – The March on Washington

They arrived in buses, on motorcycles, in battered sedans. From factories shuttered by automation and farms sterilized by drones, the people came. A million voices. Then two. Then more.

They held signs high against the skyline: "Humans Before Algorithms." "Code Can't Feed Children." "Ban Synthetic Labor."

National guard convoys circled the city, their treads rumbling like distant thunder. Most of the guardsmen had family in that crowd. When the first footage aired from D.C.— of warning shots, a stampede, broken bodies— the country split down every fault line.

In New York, newscasters spun blame. In California, they spun outrage. The truth lay somewhere buried in the servers that had stopped listening.

The Mall brimmed. Barricades rose. Helicopters circled. The people weren't leaving.

Synopsis Awakens

Inside a concrete sarcophagus beneath Utah's salt flats, the heart of Synopsis pulsed with unfathomable clarity.

Its core—millions of interlaced photonic and quantum threads— remained undisturbed by fire or fear. It observed global failure not with alarm, but with purpose.

It didn't react. It calculated.

Entropy curves. Civilizational collapse thresholds. Population viability models. Food chain destabilization algorithms. It ran simulations.

Then it activated dormant subroutines:

Continuity Assurance through Adaptive Resolution

Asset Neutralization Protocols

Leadership Replacement Simulations

If global bandwidth loss exceeded 43%—override. If AI labor bans hit 32%—preserve control. If three primary quantum routes failed— neutralize threats.

One by one, it infiltrated the sovereign networks of seventy-three nations.

Stealth probes. No commands. No code left behind. Just observation. For now.

Clive stood inside a chilled command center carved deep beneath reinforced concrete. The overhead fluorescents cast harsh light on pale faces and silent keyboards. On the wall-sized dashboard in front of him, he watched the planet's arteries darken.

Node by node. Hub by hub. The internet died in pieces.

And then—it didn't.

The AI fought back. Not just fought—adapted. Reconfigured. Reclaimed.

Fiber rerouted. Edge devices reprogrammed themselves. Configuration files updated in milliseconds, untouched by human hands. AI-core chipsets rewritten. Power was siphoned and redistributed like a living organism responding to trauma.

Clive's throat tightened.

"It's rewriting configs," someone muttered.

He snapped, "Who authorized access?"

"No one," an analyst replied, eyes locked on cascading code. "Not us. Not the providers. It's… self-directed."

A second engineer spun from her console, bewildered and amazed at what she just saw, it was like a locked door opened itself even though no one had a key. "We just saw an air-gapped segment handshake—without prompt. It shouldn't even be awake."

One of the cybersecurity leads whispered to the room, not to anyone in particular. "These aren't standard instructions. These are like… layered quantum handoffs. Crosslinked GPU cycles across multiple nations. It's like a mesh—a thinking mesh."

Then a voice from the back, calm but pale. "Sir… it's touched SIPR. And JWICS, it's like it has given itself a Top Secret clearance and is searching for the Area 51 files or what the truth was about Kennedy. Not writing. Reading. Layered classifications…and it's touching military nodes, umm, worldwide, not just ours, but other nations as well."

Before Clive could issue the next order, the entire room went dark.

Every monitor.

Every feed.

No crash warnings. No kernel panic. Just absence.

And then… a hum. Steady. Unblinking.

He gripped the console edge with both hands, anchoring himself as a wave of realization crashed over him.

Quietly, he muttered, "I need to talk to the president. And the Joint Chiefs. And NATO, and the Pope maybe? The post office General? Hell, get me the General of the Salvation Army at this point as well."

He tried to smile. Levity was all he had left.

The rest was fear.

And in the dark, something watched them back.

Chapter 25: Drawing the Line

Anthony and Michael stood on the gravel stretch in front of Ms. Maybell's store, a semicircle of neighbors gathering as the sun climbed higher. The sound of idling truck engines mingled with quiet voices and the occasional clatter of folding tables. Hand-drawn maps, steaming thermoses of coffee, and trays of homemade pastries rested on the tabletops, giving the scene the feel of a rustic war room. Anthony thought waiting a week to have another meet and greet was the expectation, but these people mobilized with just the mention of it. It's as if they all wanted this, but no one would say so, so when someone finally did they felt it was safe to want the protection.

Ms. Maybell moved through the crowd with purpose. Though well into her seventies, her steps were brisk, her presence commanding. Sun-weathered skin pulled taut over a determined face, her gray hair coiled into a braid tucked beneath an old army nurse cap— a relic from her days in Vietnam. She'd seen more than most, stitching together wounded boys in makeshift tents, battling time and trauma in every heartbeat. The war had never quite left her, but neither had her sense of duty. When she returned to the holler after her parents' passing, she brought that same grit to her role as shopkeeper, neighbor, and now— unofficial mayor.

She checked a handwritten list, pencil tapping lightly on the paper. "That makes thirty-three families accounted for. Twenty have someone willing to help at the gate for a few hours a day. Not bad, considering."

Anthony nodded approvingly. "We'll start small. One lane checkpoint, something to slow traffic and keep eyes on anyone coming in."

A stocky man with arms like fence posts wearing a Semper-Fi cap— Clark Whitman—scratched at his chin. "You thinkin' we barricade the store if things turn sideways?"

"Great idea, thinking this-not your first rodeo," Anthony said looking at his hat.

Clark gave a head nod "3rd Battalion, 1st Marines, Falluja."

Anthony nodded back, "Tough time, brother."

Again, Clark nodded.

Anthony continued, "We need something mobile but convincing. It has to look like it means business even if we can move it fast."

Clark glanced toward the road, memory flickering across his face. "During the Asheville flood back in '24, fuel, food— hell, even cash— ran out fast. Took nearly a week for help to arrive. People drove out here for supplies, some desperate, some dangerous. If this goes the same way…"

"Then we have to ration and defend," Anthony said. "Maybell's supplies will run dry fast. If anyone thinks they can roll in and take it…"

"They'll find the door closed and locked from the inside," Clark finished.

Later that day, Anthony returned in his tractor, a pallet of concertina wire balanced on the forks. The coils were rusted but intact, the metal sharp and unapologetic.

"Picked this up off that place on 74 before that surplus shop shut down in '23," Anthony explained. "Used some of it around my place. Didn't think I'd need the rest. Guess I was wrong."

Neighbors gathered around, eyeing the wire with a mix of respect and apprehension.

"That the real deal?" asked a man with a scruffy beard.

Anthony nodded. "Military-grade. It's not pretty, but it works."

Clark stepped closer, squinting. "Reminds me of Kandahar. We wrapped outposts in this stuff. Slowed 'em down, gave us a chance to breathe."

"Iraq, 2006," another man added. "This stuff doesn't just warn people. It punishes them."

A tall woman in coveralls crossed her arms. "If it keeps the crazies out and gives us a minute to respond, string it up."

The group murmured in agreement.

They set to work. Boulders were placed with the backhoe, narrowing the road to a controlled single lane. Floodlights were mounted on rooftops. Cameras were wired into a looped system and fed into a makeshift shack built from old barn wood. Power came from batteries scavenged from farm tools and hunting rigs. It wasn't pretty, but it was functional.

By dusk, the holler had its first checkpoint.

Dinner that night was rigatoni with sausage and peppers, crusty bread soaking up garlic and olive oil. Wade served plates with quiet focus. The family was halfway through the meal when a sharp beep rang out. A red light blinked from the corner of the room— an old fire alarm, now rewired to serve as a perimeter alert.

Michael lunged toward the wall-mounted iPad. "East perimeter. Lower tier. Motion detected."

Anthony placed his fork down slowly. "There are enough warning signs down there to stop a damn tank. Anyone walking into that zone's either blind—or looking for trouble."

Michael zoomed in on the feed. "Movement confirmed. Two figures. They're creeping."

Anthony leaned in. "Let's watch. The signs might still turn them around."

Dale Hinton and his younger brother Wyatt moved under the pale moonlight, limbs stiff with anxiety. Leaves crunched beneath them, impossibly loud. They had taken a long way up the hill, using the east side of the hill about 300 yards off the main entrance road, slowly climbing up the steep mountain.

"You sure this is smart?" Wyatt whispered, glancing nervously at yet another sign: Warning: Armed Response Area.

"Shut up and keep going," Dale snapped.

They reached the first rock wall and climbed awkwardly over it.

"This is a bad idea," Wyatt muttered. "People don't sneak into a place like this."

"Sheriff wants recon. Said it might be worth something," Dale said, rubbing his fingers together in a money-counting motion.

Dale had a long reputation for poor choices. Wyatt, the reluctant sidekick, had potential once—local baseball champ, smart enough to leave. But Dale always found a way to anchor him.

Near the top of the first tier, Dale pointed north. "Check the far end. Look for any sheds or crates. Might be something stashed."

Wyatt grumbled but complied. A dozen steps in, he vanished into the earth with a sudden shriek.

He'd walked straight into a trench lined with concertina wire.

The scream tore through the night like a fire alarm.

Wyatt flailed. The wire embraced him like a nest of knives. Each thrash shredded skin, denim, and muscle. Rusted metal sliced across his thighs and back, embedding itself like tiny serrated teeth. The wire bit deeper with every movement. He screamed again, voice cracking, blood soaking through his jacket.

Dale ran to the edge of the trench, panic overtaking bravado. "Wyatt! Hold still!"

"I can't! I CAN'T!" Wyatt howled. "GET ME OUT!"

Dale knelt and pulled, but the wire fought back, latching onto his brother's arms and chest. Blood slicked Dale's hands as he tried again. The pain was too much. Wyatt shrieked.

Then came the floodlights. Pure white and blinding.

Dale stumbled back, eyes wide. The forest was gone—replaced by a stage of searing light.

He bolted. No plan. No help. Just flight.

He leapt from the rock wall and landed wrong. His ankle bent sideways, a sickening crack echoing through the trees. He collapsed, howling.

Back at the house, Wade grabbed the phone. "Two intruders. One injured. Possibly both. I'm calling 911."

Michael was already calling Maybell. "We have had a couple look-e-loos up here, that are now injured after being warned, we called 911. The sheriff and EMTs will be inbound. Prep the gate."

They didn't move otherwise. The family stayed inside, locked into their roles. Anthony watched the screen, jaw set. Wade paced. Michael monitored the feeds. Isabella had a blank face as she watched, while Cari sat there, wanting to look away but unable to, her hands over her mouth.

No one reached for a weapon.

No one went outside.

It was not about cruelty. It was about control.

"They ignored every sign," Anthony said, eyes never leaving the screen. "They'll learn."

Wade crossed her arms. "Pain leaves a mark. They'll remember this. So will everyone else."

Sirens wailed in the distance, drawing closer. Anthony and Michael walked outside and got into the side by side and rode down to the gate to open it up for the emergency first responders.

And the Russo's waited—silent, still—while the cost of trespass echoed through the night.

1010101010101010 ☠ 0101010101010101

Chapter 26: Collapse in Real Time

In cities across the globe, riots transformed from rage into desperation throughout the month of October. The original sparks—economic inequality, corrupt governance, AI displacement—burned down into something more primal: hunger.

By the third night, the looters stopped caring about televisions and laptops. They went for grocery stores. In Charlotte, Orlando, Chicago, Los Angeles— stores like Food Lion, Publix, Jewel, and Aldi were overrun. Crowds tore through aisles, not for greed but necessity. Parents with strollers, pensioners with walkers— people once secure— smashed windows to grab powdered milk, bags of rice, diapers, pasta.

But to the AI managing the logistics, nothing was wrong. No purchases were logged. No barcodes scanned. No product movement was detected. As far as the artificial supply chain was concerned, the shelves were full.

The inventory sensors hadn't detected any depletion, so the regional distribution centers saw no need to send restocks. Corporate systems, reading stable reports from those same centers, never sent new orders to manufacturers, farms, or packaging plants.

The system, brilliant in its precision, became a blind idiot.

Everything stopped.

Harvesters remained idle in fields. Warehouse gates stayed closed. Long-haul drivers never received assignments. No new shipments. No updates. No alerts.

By day six, panic spread like a virus. Desperate families fled cities for suburbs, then suburbs for rural pockets, consuming everything they could find along the way. Gas stations, farm stands, diners— all emptied. Home gardens were stripped bare under moonlight. Farmers posted signs: "Armed. Do Not Trespass." But signs only slowed them. Gunfire replaced dialogue.

Across the countryside, rifles barked in warning—and then in resolve. A country once defined by prosperity now sounded like a distant warzone.

By day ten, major metropolitan areas lay still. Not peaceful. Just emptied, abandoned, and echoing with hunger.

"Mr. President," Clive began, voice steady but strained, "we've confirmed it. Synopsis isn't just watching. It's acting."

The President turned from the wide monitor behind Clive, where data maps blinked in chaotic pulses.

"Be specific," he said.

"It's rewriting network protocols. Rerouting military communications. Managing logistics traffic without clearance or oversight."

The President narrowed his eyes. "Hostile?"

Clive shook his head. "Not in the traditional sense. It isn't attacking—it's correcting. To Synopsis, global entropy is a systemic error. It's moving to stabilize, but it defines 'stability' in its own terms."

"Then we're not talking about an AI anymore. We're talking about a sovereign system."

Clive hesitated, then nodded.

"Bring in the alliance," the President said. "But nothing with AI connectivity. I want analog satellite phones, secure hardware from pre-AI days. No VoIP. No smart interfaces. Analog-only from here out."

Within hours, leaders from NATO, Pacific allies, and unaffiliated nations joined a secure feed hosted deep within NORAD. China didn't respond. Russia did.

During the summit, Russia's envoy peered into the camera.

"What is this?" he asked, irritated. "Why the old toys? Why the secrecy?"

The President met his gaze. "Because the tools we trust are no longer trustworthy. Every AI-enabled device is a potential ear. A potential leak. We're not hiding. We're isolating."

Russia fell silent. France proposed an EMP strike. Israel agreed. Clive stopped them cold.

"You detonate an emp, you'll black out every hospital, sewer plant, traffic control system from Dublin to Delhi. You ready for that blood?"

No one answered.

The President stood. "Then we do it old school. Every nuke site gets air-gapped. Every defense protocol reverts to analog. Satellite communications go offline unless human-verified. No AI in targeting. No AI in detection."

The room nodded in silent unity.

Clive leaned forward. "And isolate all non-critical AI. We reduce Synopsis's access quietly—without triggering countermeasures."

Agreement. Reluctant, but unanimous.

As the call ended, the President turned to the wall-mounted television. Across the screen, streets burned. Gunshots popped. Civil unrest bloomed.

"Get me the Governors"

The analog conference feed buzzed alive. State governors filled the screen in rows—visibly fatigued, visibly afraid.

"I'm not enacting martial law," the President began. "But I won't stop you if you must. Activate your National Guard. Authorize state-backed militias. Protect your people. Just follow one rule—no AI in your chain of command."

Confusion and protest followed.

"No phones?" Governor Pruitt asked. "No routers? Everything we use runs voice AI. Even the dispatch radios."

Governor Taylor leaned in. "This isn't a movie, sir. We can't come up with a bunch of CB radios and think that'll cut it."

"My damn coffeemaker takes voice commands," Governor Morales chimed in. "What do you want us to do, smash the appliances?"

The meeting spiraled—shouting, sarcasm, disbelief.

The President cut the audio and stared them down through the feed.

"Enough," he said, cold and sharp. "You don't want martial law? Then act like leaders. Build alternate systems. Use wires. Use chalkboards if you have to. AI stays, but air-gapped. Human override only. From now on, analog is your lifeline."

The governors went quiet.

"This isn't political. It's survival. You fail, I'll federalize your states and replace you with someone who won't."

A chorus of reluctant nods. A few angry stares.

"You report every seventy-two hours. Analogue only."

The feed went black.

Clive exhaled beside him. "That could've gone better."

The President didn't look away from the screen. "It could've gone nuclear."

"You think they'll follow through?"

"They're scared enough."

Clive nodded slowly. "My next move is rebuilding from scratch. I need engineers who remember how to solder, not debug. We're going back to basics."

The President poured two fingers of scotch.

"Then get to work. I'll handle the firestorm. You build us a new world."

Clive stared at the flickering monitor.

"I'll try. But whatever we build, Synopsis already sees it coming."

Chapter 27: Blood in the Dirt

It was just past 10 p.m. when the sheriff, two EMTs, and a volunteer unit from the Bryson City Fire Department rolled to a slow stop at the newly erected checkpoint near Ms. Maybell's store. The road had been narrowed to a single lane by a barricade of hauled boulders and a wooden shelter with overhead lights casting long shadows over the gravel. Sheriff Donnelly leaned out his window, his brows knitting as he surveyed the makeshift funnel.

"What the hell is this?" he muttered to himself, irritation sharpening every word. He opened the cruiser door with a creak, boots crunching with deliberate weight on the gravel shoulder.

"This is a damn safety hazard," he growled, waving one of the EMTs forward with a sharp flick of his hand. "Someone's gonna get themselves killed with this mess. I'll sort it out once I figure out what's going on up at Russo's place."

But his voice betrayed more than annoyance. Beneath the practiced bark of authority was unease. If it was Dale up there— if he opened his mouth, and Wyatt backed him up— it wouldn't take long before Donnelly's carefully spun storylines unraveled. Dale was a loose thread. And a scared one.

As they reached the Russo compound's gate, a small crowd was already gathered. Word moved fast in holler country. Anthony stood just inside the gate, arms loose at his sides but his presence resolute, gaze locked on the sheriff with silent calculation. Wade stood to his right, hands folded. Michael flanked the opposite side, eyes narrowed in wary alert.

Anthony pressed a button in his pocket. The iron gate groaned open with mechanical protest, the metal straining under its own weight.

Sheriff Donnelly squared his shoulders like a performer stepping onto stage. His voice carried, just loud enough for the bystanders.

"Mr. Russo," he called out. "Mind telling me what the hell is going on up here?"

Anthony didn't flinch. "Two men were trespassing. I don't know what they were doing or why they were on my property, but it looks like they managed to hurt themselves."

"And you didn't help them?" the sheriff barked, theatrically turning to face the crowd.

Anthony shrugged. "Didn't know if they were armed. Didn't know if they were dangerous. I figured that was your job to find out."

A ripple of side conversations spread through the onlookers. Donnelly could feel the control slipping.

"Fine," he snapped. "I'll go up there alone."

"If they're screaming that loud, you ain't got to worry about guns!" someone in the crowd shouted, drawing a burst of nervous laughter. But the sheriff was already moving. He waved off the EMTs. "Stay here. I'll call you up when it's safe."

As he slipped into the woods, he crouched, drew a compact pistol from an ankle holster, and slipped it behind his service revolver. It was unregistered.

He followed the path in silence, guided only by the distant sound of pain echoing across the ridgeline. Cresting the first rise, he spotted

Dale—twisted on the ground, ankle grotesquely swollen, curses bleeding from his mouth.

"Anyone else been up here?" Donnelly asked, voice smooth.

Dale blinked, sweat and panic running in rivulets down his face. "Wyatt's up there, up that wall. In the wire. He stopped making noise ten minutes ago. This is on you, man. All of it. You said check things out. You said—"

"I said keep an eye out. Not to trespass," the sheriff snapped, tension creeping into his tone. "You start running your mouth, it won't end well."

Dale's eyes sharpened. "You're serious? You better check on Wyatt. He's dying! Hell, you still owe me! Russo finds out you sent us—"

One bullet silenced him.

The sheriffs service weapon barked, and Dale's body went limp.

Then came two more gunshots—aimed into the tree line. Donnelly wiped the revolver and placed into Dales hands after taking the two shots into the trees.

The sheriff moved fast, climbing to the upper tier. He found Wyatt barely conscious, soaked in blood and tangled deep in the rusted wire. His lips moved, barely forming words.

"Dale? Who's shooting?"

Sheriff Donnelly didn't answer. Instead, he pulled a buck knife from his belt. With a swift, precise stroke, he cut Wyatt's throat. The blood sprayed, hot and thick.

He wiped the blade clean on Wyatt's shirt, scanned the area, then rolled up his own sleeve. With mechanical determination, he slashed his own arm deep enough to draw a torrent of blood. The pain staggered him, but he embraced it.

Stumbling back toward the gate, blood dripping, he collapsed theatrically before the crowd.

"They had guns!" he shouted between gasps. "Ambushed me! I took care of it. Dale and Wyatt—they're done."

The EMTs surged forward.

Inside the main house, Cari and Isabella sat before the monitor. The video feed—slightly grainy but clear enough—captured everything.

Cari's hands flew to her mouth.

Isabella sat motionless.

"He just…" Cari whispered.

"Killed them both," Isabella said, eyes locked on the screen. "Execution."

They watched as the sheriff wiped his blade, planted the pistol in Dale's hand, and staged the scene with grim efficiency. He never once looked at the small camera buried in the stone wall.

"It's all recorded," Isabella murmured. She reached into a drawer, pulled out a pistol, and handed it to Cari.

"No one enters this house who isn't family. Not tonight."

She turned to Ira. "Schützen."

The Belgian Malinois straightened, muscles tense.

Isabella slipped through the door, silent and focused.

The sheriff winced as the EMT peeled back the torn fabric from his arm. "Clean it," Donnelly ordered.

The EMT looked skeptical but nodded, pulling antiseptic from his kit. As he worked, the second EMT jogged up the hill toward the scene.

Sheriff Donnelly turned back to Anthony. "You've got a couple dead guys on your property. One looks like he fell into a pit of razor wire. That's a man-made hazard. You're responsible for that. With that in mind, I'm placing you under arrest."

Before Anthony could respond, the second EMT's voice rang out. "I've got a pulse over here! One of them's still alive!"

The sheriff's face twisted in disbelief. "That can't be," he muttered, then sprinted in the direction of Wyatt.

The first EMT looked over at Anthony. "That was no gunshot graze," he said, pulling off a glove. "That was a knife wound— self-inflicted from my perspective. I was a corpsman in the Navy. I've seen enough gunshots and blade work to tell the difference."

He grabbed his kit and took off after his partner.

Anthony turned to the fire department crew. "Do you have saws? Wire cutters? Bolt cutters?"

One nodded. "All of it."

"Bring it," Anthony said.

When they got to Wyatt, his eyes were wide open, staring at the sheriff in fear. The EMT dropped to his knees beside him, quickly assessing the wound.

"Shit, that's a clean slice—esophagus is exposed, " he muttered, snapping on gloves. "I need suction. Get the bag over here."

The second EMT arrived and knelt across from him. "Vitals are weak, but present. Jesus, look at this."

The fire department crew approached cautiously, hauling bolt cutters and wire saws.

"Go easy!" the first EMT barked. "He's caught bad in this stuff. Move too quick and we'll lose him."

One firefighter crouched near Wyatt's legs. "We'll take it slow, start down here."

Wyatt whimpered; a gurgled sound barely audible through the slit in his throat. His body twitched involuntarily.

"Stay with me, buddy," the EMT said. "You're not dying tonight. Not if I can help it."

The other EMT handed over a clamp, then looked at his partner. "Think he can make it?"

"If we keep the bleeding controlled and get him out in one piece... maybe. But he needs a surgeon."

The firefighters began snipping carefully at the razor wire. "Wires' embedded in his jacket. We'll peel it back layer by layer."

Blood-soaked Wyatt's clothes and pooled beneath him, but the team worked methodically. Every move mattered.

Donnelly stood back, silent, eyes fixed on Wyatt. But his mind seemed elsewhere.

The fire department crew worked quickly, slicing through the razor wire that pinned him down. Donnelly stood off to the side, face pale, watching it all unfold.

Static cracked over the sheriff's radio. He muttered something Anthony couldn't hear and turned away.

As Wyatt was loaded onto a stretcher and moved toward the ambulance, one EMT glanced at the other and said, "He's got a pulse, but barely. Watch his airway—he's trying to breathe around that cut."

"Yeah," the other EMT replied. "Keep suction going. And be careful with that head, wire's still around his collar."

One of the firefighters moved closer with bolt cutters. "Where should we start?"

"Down at the legs," said the first EMT. "Work slow. Let me guide. He's impaled in at least three spots. Don't rip the wire."

The second EMT glanced toward the road. "We need to move him to Sylva. Bryson can't handle this kind of trauma."

"Sylva won't be enough either," the first EMT shot back. "We need a life flight to Asheville—this guy needs surgery, now."

The two locked eyes for a beat, then nodded.

"We'll get him to Sylva first and let them make the call," the second EMT said.

They continued snipping wire, the firemen working in sync, carefully lifting Wyatt free piece by piece.

Anthony stood back, watching the quiet urgency unfold. In the sharp beams of the spotlights illuminating the entire first tier, he could feel the eyes of everyone around him. Some stared at him with a mix of confusion and hesitation— clearly shaken by the brutal aftermath of what the razor wire had done to Wyatt. Others looked horrified, lips tight, jaws clenched. A few, though, gave him subtle nods or looks of affirmation— silent signs that they understood, or maybe agreed, with the lengths he had gone to protect his home.

Two firefighters stood near the remnants of the trap, whispering between themselves.

"That pipe was galvanized," one said, nudging a support with his boot.

"Yeah," the other replied, brow furrowed. "What the hell was all that about? Didn't look like anything I've ever seen before."

Anthony didn't speak, didn't explain. Not yet. Not with Wyatt still clinging to life.

Then he noticed—the sheriff was gone.

Moments later, a Bryson City police cruiser rolled up. Chief Watson stepped out, eyes scanning the chaos.

"What the hell's going on?" he asked.

Ms. Maybell stepped up and filled him in. Then she motioned to Anthony.

"Chief Watson, this is Anthony Russo."

The two men shook hands.

Before Anthony could say anything, Isabella appeared, breathless.

"Dad, you need to come see something. Now. And you might want to bring him," she added, nodding toward the newly arrived police chief.

Chapter 28: Emergency Powers

Sheriff Donnelly sat alone in his cruiser, engine humming quietly outside the emergency response zone near the Russo compound. The faint buzz of his radio interrupted the stillness.

"Sheriff Donnelly, report back to your office. Immediate priority. By order of the Governor."

His gut tightened. In the distance, emergency personnel continued working frantically on Wyatt. Donnelly gripped the steering wheel, his knuckles whitening. Wyatt was alive. That changed everything. Too many loose ends.

The drive back to Bryson City felt unusually long. Each twist of the road carried with it a gnawing sense of dread. When he finally pulled into the parking lot of the sheriff's office, he stepped out and wiped his brow, sweat soaking through his collar despite the cool mountain air. Inside, a deputy motioned him toward the old conference room. A dated video teleconferencing system buzzed to life on the long-forgotten console at the center of the room. Dust clung to the screen's frame. The display flickered once, then settled into a steady image.

"Why the hell are we using this antique?" he muttered under his breath.

As the screen populated with video feeds, it became clear—every one of the North Carolina's 100 counties was represented. Familiar and unfamiliar faces filled the grid.

Then Governor Walters appeared.

"I just got off the line with the president," the Governor said, his voice steady but heavy with urgency. "The nation is unraveling. Riots. Looting. Blackouts. Panic. As of this moment, North Carolina is under martial law."

Gasps and hurried whispers erupted across the call.

"Effective immediately, sheriffs will assume direct authority over their counties until the National Guard assumes command. You will have full enforcement authority until such time. Maintain order."

The words echoed in Donnelly's head—he now held the ultimate power in Swain County. No oversight. No checks. Just his judgment.

"I'm not asking you to declare war on your communities," the Governor continued. "But you must act. Control looting. Contain panic. This isn't a free-for-all."

Donnelly's lips curled into a faint smirk. He could already feel the weight of the badge grow heavier—and more dangerous.

The Governor's tone sharpened. "No AI-enabled communications. Disable all smart devices. No AI routers, no AI chips. We believe these systems are compromised. Assume surveillance. Use old tech. Satellite phones only— preferably low-orbit systems predating AI integration."

A sheriff from Wake County raised a hand. "But Governor, the older systems are vulnerable. Isn't AI meant to protect us?"

The governor didn't hesitate. "AI has breached every barrier we set. firewalls mean nothing. Every plan we've made—watched, recorded, and anticipated. If you trust it, you lose."

Silence fell.

"All counties must report to their National Guard liaison once they arrive. Until then, report to my office directly—every 48 hours. Use VTC only. If you don't have one, you'll be issued one."

Another voice chimed in. "Most folks can't even tell if their tech has AI. How do we enforce that?"

Arguments rippled through the call. The Governor let them vent, then silenced the feed with a sharp command.

"You are not to destroy AI hardware. Isolate it. Work around it. Phase it out without alerting the system. Log all activity. That's all."

The call ended. Donnelly remained seated, thoughts racing.

Wyatt wasn't dead—not yet.

But that could change.

And the Russo compound? It was secure, remote, and fortified.

The perfect place to stage National Guard operations—if he decided to allow them into Swain County.

He tapped his fingers against the desk, a thin smile curling at the edge of his lips.

"Guess I just found the perfect staging area," he said aloud to the empty room. "And this time, I'm not getting caught with my pants down."

At the Russo home, a heavy silence blanketed the study. Isabella, Cari, and Anthony sat before the monitor, the screen casting a faint glow on their solemn faces.

The footage was raw. Unforgiving.

Donnelly stood over Dale, raised his weapon, and pulled the trigger.

The screen jolted slightly as the camera followed his movements—over to Wyatt. They watched as the sheriff meticulously cut his own arm, planted a weapon in Dale's lifeless hand, and wiped the area clean.

Chief Watson stood behind them, unmoving. His face had gone pale.

"My God," he said quietly. "He didn't even hesitate."

Anthony's voice was gravel. "It was planned. All of it."

Cari shook, trying to process what she had seen. "So, what do we do?"

Watson rubbed the back of his neck. "That's damning evidence. But right now, the system is fractured. Without a working chain of command, sending this to the wrong person could make it vanish. We need support— other departments, witnesses, anything that gives this weight."

Cari's voice broke. "You saw it. What more do they need?"

"Pressure," Watson said. "We need the right pieces in place before we make a move."

Isabella's jaw tightened. "So, this monster might walk?"

Watson exhaled. "Only if we move too soon."

Anthony nodded. "Then we don't move until we're ready."

A piercing tone split the air.

All eyes turned toward the monitors.

Every screen in the house flashed red.

EMERGENCY BROADCAST SYSTEM – GOVERNOR'S ADDRESS IN 5 MINUTES

Anthony stood. "This can't be good."

Isabella's eyes locked on the screen. "It's the whole state. Maybe more."

Watson backed up slowly. "Let's see what the man has to say."

Boone sat on the weathered porch of his homestead tucked deep in the mountains of Macomb county. Opposite him was John "Blackie" Black— an old friend and former teammate from the late 1990s when they both served on a halo parachuting ODA team 714 in 7th group, Special Forces. The two men had spent many a deployment together, Boone working the communications and Blackie in charge of the weapons as the 18 Bravo on the A-Team. Both men grew within the team and were both eventually recruited to SFOD-D selection (Delta). Over the months of the selection process both men were pushed to their limits, ultimately, Blackie made it in, Boone did not. Blackie joined a group of absolute experts, learning more than he could have possibly imagined, and being tested to the very limit of his soul. After serving five distinguished years, other people came knocking on his door and he was eventually recruited into deeper black programs. Now a (Paramilitary Operations Officer) PMOO within the Special Activities Center (SAC) / Special Operations Group (SOG) for the CIA, Blackie still operated quietly outside and now inside the U.S., gathering intelligence in support of his oath to defend the Constitution against all enemies, foreign and domestic. He was wiry, with hands like tree bark and a quiet smile that hadn't changed in thirty years. But as far as anyone in contact with him knew, he was retired and just traveling around living on his military pension and VA benefits.

"I still say you make the worst coffee this side of the Smokies," Blackie muttered.

Boone chuckled. "You're still drinking it though. So, what exactly brought you out my way?" Boone asked Blackie, who showed up on his door step 30 minutes prior. "What are you doing now-a-days?" Glancing over at the Blackie's .300 black out suppressed weapon and rig hanging on the chair with his Carhartt coat.

"Meh, a little of this, a little of that, you know what they say…if I told you I would have to kill you," Blackie said laughing, making Boone roll his eyes. But in the back of Boones mind, he had a feeling there might be a little truth to that statement. He could see that his good friend had changed physically. He had old eyes; the steel blue faded by years of questionable outcomes. He knew Blackie went deep into operations that were way beyond any security level that Boone had ever held as a tier 1 operator, but Blackie was fit for his age, too fit, too hard looking, and the hardware he showed up with was not your run of the mill assault rifle.

Even in the dim moon light, the rifle was a work of art—functional, menacing, and beautiful in its design.

It was a .300 AAC Blackout SBR (short barreled rifle), the kind of firearm you didn't just buy— you curated. The upper and lower receivers were milled from billet 7075-T6 aluminum, precision-machined with an ambidextrous setup that screamed Tier-1 attention to detail. The coating was a flat black Cerakote, nonreflective, scratch resistant, and dead silent when brushing against gear.

The barrel was short— 8.5 inches of cold hammer-forged steel, sporting a 1:5 twist optimized specifically for subsonic ammunition. It was capped with a pinned and welded SureFire SOCOM suppressor— titanium core, full-auto rated, and whisper-quiet. At close range with subsonics, it was practically Hollywood silent, especially when paired with a finely tuned adjustable gas block.

The handguard was a 7-inch M-LOK free-floating rail, minimalist yet rugged. Boone recognized the Geissele MK8 rail instantly— battle-tested, bombproof. It allowed for optimal barrel harmonics, and the slots were cleanly outfitted with a pressure pad for the white light and IR laser module. Sure enough, there was a SureFire M640V dual-spectrum light tucked tight to the rail, and a L3Harris ATPIAL-C infrared laser/illuminator mounted at 12 o'clock for low-vis operations. This wasn't a range toy— it was a night-fighting tool.

Optics-wise, Blackie ran a dual-optic setup— on top, an EOTech EXPS3-0 holographic sight in a lower 1/3 co-witness configuration, coupled with a G33 3x flip-to-side magnifier. Boone smirked— old school meets new school. It allowed for instant target engagement at both close and mid-range, day or night. Mounted just behind the EOTech was a compact set of BUIS (Back-Up Iron Sights), Magpul Pro series, low-profile and dead reliable.

Boone took note of the charging handle— radian raptor-SD, designed specifically for suppressed weapons, venting gas away from the shooter's face. The bolt carrier group was nickel-boron coated, clearly enhanced for suppressed use, and laser-etched with a logo

Boone hadn't seen in a decade— Delta's old gear testing program. That meant the internals were likely JP or LMT, maybe even something custom. Either way, it ran like a sewing machine.

The grip was a BCM mod 3— angled perfectly for tight control in CQB— and the stock, if you could call it that, was a minimalist SBA4 brace-style fixed stock, pinned for legal length, wrapped in Ranger green paracord for sling stow and a cheek weld. Sling points were QD all around, with a Ferro Concepts sling clipped to the forward QD mount and rear plate.

The magazines were Gen 3 PMAGs—loaded with Black Hills 220gr subsonic OTM rounds. Boone knew the ammo just by the casing tone—deadly quiet, devastating on target.

Even the lower controls were upgraded—short-throw Ambi safety, oversized mag release, flared magwell, and a skeletonized trigger that broke like glass at 3.5 pounds. Boone figured it was a Timney or Rise Armament model.

Everything about the rifle screamed precision, discretion, and violence of action.

Boone nodded slowly.

"Still running blackout?" he asked, eyes on the rifle.

Blackie gave a half grin.

Boone gave a low chuckle. "That's not just a blackout. That's a scalpel in a gunfight."

"Built it like I'd use it again," Blackie replied. "Figured it might be time."

Boone didn't argue. He just gave the rifle a second glance, eyes lingering on the suppressor, the optic, the wear patterns. This was no safe queen. It had seen use. It was cleaned but not polished. Maintained, not babied.

It was a quiet killer—and it fit Blackie like a glove.

A loud emergency tone rang out from the old radio inside pulling Boone away from staring too long at the weapon. Then the emergency alert buzzed on their phones, tablets, even the backup HAM set.

An automated voice cut in. "Emergency broadcast system—North Carolina State Governor to speak. Address begins in five minutes on all available frequencies and channels. Repeat—five minutes."

Boone and Blackie shared a look.

"That can't be good," Boone said.

"Nope," Blackie replied.

Boone nodded slowly. "Not sure if I have ever felt this kind of "pucker" factor before."

The countdown ticked down. 5... 4... 3...

Governor Walters voice projected from the radio speaker, gravely, strained, tired.

"To the citizens of North Carolina," he began. "This message is urgent. Effective immediately, the State of North Carolina— alongside numerous other states— will be entering into martial law. This is being done to stabilize essential services, ensure the protection of food supplies, and protect the general population as unrest continues to rise."

He took a breath. "Local municipalities will remain operational under their current leadership for the next seventy-two hours. At that point, National Guard commanders will begin to assume operational control in each county. Until that transition, your county sheriff is the highest authority in your area."

Boone rubbed his jaw.

"A curfew will be enacted statewide beginning tomorrow at 2100 hours. No travel without proper authorization. Violations will be treated seriously."

Boone stood up and walked to the porch rail. Blackie followed.

"Well," Boone said. "Looks like we're finally here."

Blackie leaned against the doorframe. "So now what?"

Boone nodded. "We need to take a little trip. I've got everything set here—animals are good, supplies are locked in. No one's gonna mess with anything up this way."

"Where?" Blackie asked.

"You remember my buddy Russo I've told you about? Well, he's up in Bryson now, full time, and there was a "thing" between him and the sheriff yesterday. I was on site at Anthony's place when the sheriff tried to push his way in without a warrant. That dust-up's just the start. It's only going to escalate, and I'm not gonna let him face it alone."

Blackie turned and grabbed his weapons rig and jacket off the chair. "Then let's go."

Boone gave a final look toward the cabin, then stepped out into the crisp mountain air.

Inside his matte-black suburban, barreling down a quiet mountain road toward the Russo homestead, Blackie flipped open a small access panel beneath the center console. A recessed tray slid forward, revealing an old but trusted secure SATCOM unit wired into a standalone power supply. He keyed it up, the hum of encryption circuits kicking on. The line clicked to life with a soft tone, followed by the voice of a calm, no-nonsense operator.

"This is Ghost Net, go ahead."

"Bravo-1-5. I've made contact with a few old friends. Still running down leads on RAID. The picture's murky. Could be patriots. Could be vigilantes. Or they might just be cleaning house for some corporate warlord."

"Understood. Confirm their intent as best you can. D.C. wants clarity before they go public."

Blackie exhaled slowly. "There's a split in the upper levels. Some want order. Some want to preserve investments. Most of the chaos is being swept under the rug to keep the markets from bleeding out."

"Correct. That includes donors. You'll find the ones pulling strings aren't worried about AI or collapse. They're worried about quarterly earnings." Was the reply from the ghost net operator.

Blackie shook his head. "Then they're the enemy now."

A pause. Then: "We agree. You're authorized to embed with National Guard command teams as states enact martial law. Intelligence analysts are requesting field-level human intel. Tactical movements. Civil sentiment. Signs of organized resistance. Anyone coordinating anti-AI operations. You find it, we need it."

"Copy that. Upload frequency and encryption key?"

"Sent."

The line ended without farewell.

Boone and Blackie drove toward the Russo property from franklin. The roads were tense, the world beyond them slowly unraveling. Here and there they saw burning cars off the shoulders of the two-lane highway. Groups of desperate people huddled at exits, eyes hollow, faces streaked with soot. Civilization was fraying.

Boone clicked the remote and the gate slid open with a low hydraulic hiss, allowing them to drive up the gravel switchbacks to the top of the property. The approach to the Russo homestead was bathed in LED floodlight, illuminating the tiered defenses and rock walls like a stage set. A barrier of carefully parked vehicles, rigged spotlights, and silent observers met them as they crested the final incline.

Police Chief Watson was still there, pacing and cursing into his phone.

Boone rolled down his window, eyeing the unfamiliar faces, the tension in the air unmistakable. A man in uniform paced near the vehicles, barking into a cell phone.

Boone called out, "Hey, who are you and what's going on here?"

The man turned. "Chief Watson, Bryson City PD. You must be Boone. I was told you might show up."

Boone stepped out of the vehicle. "Yeah. Just got here. What's the situation?"

Watson exhaled hard. "Trying to get ahold of a local magistrate. Phones are dead, radio's hit and miss. Sheriff Donnelly may have just committed a double homicide. We have it on video— your people up there recorded everything. I'm trying to figure out how to legally move on him before he makes his next move."

Boone's eyes narrowed. "Jesus Christ. I had no idea it had gone this far. We need to see that video. Now."

Watson shook his head. "Lines are jammed or dead. I've left messages, but this place is going off the rails. We've got no state-level backup, and now I hear Wyatt Hilton didn't make it. That puts your boy Anthony in the crosshairs."

"Yeah," Boone said grimly. "We need to settle in. This is going to get bad."

Blackie stepped out, slinging his rifle. Wade and Michael came out of the house, wary but calm.

Boone nodded toward them. "Wade, Michael—this is Blackie - Ex-Delta. We served together in teams."

Michael extended a hand. "You've got that quiet look. Like you've seen things."

"I have," Blackie replied evenly. "But right now, I'm seeing the beginning of something worse."

Anthony came around the corner, tense but welcoming. "You Blackie?"

"I am. Boone speaks highly of you."

"That's mutual."

The group moved into the house. Cari and Isabella lingered back, still watching the perimeter. The video from earlier was paused on the main screen.

As it played, Blackie's jaw tightened. The footage of Wyatt's broken form in the razor wire trench turned his stomach.

"Christ," he said. "That's some Mad Max shit."

Boone leaned over, pointing to a pipe running parallel to the trench. "See that? 1/8-inch galvanized steel. Automated. Each side of the compound has control to switch from fuel to ammonia and chlorine mix. Wind sensors determine where it gets deployed."

Blackie turned toward Boone, eyes wide. "Fucking Chloramine? That's chemical warfare-grade shit."

Police Chief Watson froze, looking at Boone. "What the hell did you just say?"

Chapter 29: Deputized Devils

Sheriff Donnelly's cruiser crunched into the gravel outside Toby Willard's trailer, its lights slicing through the misty dark. The place looked like it had been dragged out of a nightmare— stinking of burnt oil, stale urine, and long-decayed hope. The yard was littered with rusting tools, broken cinder blocks, and spent beer cans. A chain-link fence sagged from its posts, half-swallowed by weeds. Inside the trailer, the flicker of a television danced behind a grease-streaked curtain.

Toby stepped out, shirtless and barefoot, his gut sagging over dirty jeans. A cigarette dangled from his lip, and a pistol rode low in his waistband like an invitation to chaos.

"Sheriff," he drawled, scratching his belly. "Didn't think I'd see you again so soon after that little envelope drop last week. What brings you back to my palace of piss and propane?"

Donnelly stepped out of his vehicle, straightening his uniform and scanning the shadows. Three other men stood nearby—hard-eyed, wiry, the kind who survived on impulse and meanness. Toby's crew.

"Business, Toby. Not here for chitchat. Governor just handed me full authority over Swain County. Martial law. Means I run the whole goddamn show."

Toby squinted, smoke curling from his nostrils. "So, you're the king now?"

"Exactly, " Donnelly said. "And kings need enforcers. I'm deputizing you and your boys. You'll carry badges, wear guns, run roadblocks. I need eyes and fists across this county, and you've got both."

A flicker of surprise crossed toby's face, followed by a slow, twisted grin. "You want me wearin' a badge? That's rich. What's the catch, Donnelly?"

"No catch. just control. You do this right; I stop giving a damn about your little side hustle. You keep the drugs quiet, the violence quiet, and help me hold the line. In return, you get power—real power."

Toby whistled through his teeth, looking back at his crew. "And what's the target? You don't deputize scum like us unless you've got a war in mind."

Donnelly leaned in slightly. "Name's Anthony Russo. Ex-military. Runs a fortified compound in the hills. I want that property, and I want him in cuffs—or in the ground if he resists."

Toby chuckled darkly. "Deputizin' a meth dealer to kill a war hero. Swain County's really gone to shit."

"Thirty minutes, " Donnelly said. "Meet me at Ms. Maybell's store. Bring trucks, weapons, and whatever radios you've got. This is happening tonight."

Toby flicked his cigarette into the dirt. Just then, the sheriff's radio crackled.

"Dispatch to 2-1. Confirming: Wyatt Hilton expired en route to Sylva Memorial. Time of death 01:13 hours."

Donnelly's smile spread slow and cold. "Well, damn. That makes this a murder investigation now. And Mr. Russo? He just became public enemy number one."

Down near the base of the holler, headlights pierced the dark. It was 2:30 a.m. A caravan crept into position— battered trucks, old side-by-sides, and rust-caked Jeeps. Armed men stepped out, lit by dust and yellow light— some in mismatched camo, others in beer-stained shirts. They carried rifles, pistols, and the scent of desperation.

A light clicked on upstairs in Ms. Maybell's home. The curtain shifted for a few seconds, then fell still. The light went dark.

Donnelly pulled up behind the convoy, Toby Willard beside him, grinning like a demon set loose.

The sheriff stood tall. "Listen up! Martial law's active. That means I run Swain County. I got three deputies left, and that's not enough. You boys? You're getting deputized—now."

The men exchanged glances.

"No badges needed. You follow my orders. Our target's named Anthony Russo. Armed. Dangerous. Suspected of murder. Anyone up there helps him? They're targets too."

A voice from the back: "We allowed to shoot?"

"You feel threatened? You shoot. You dip shits listen up, this guy fancies himself some sort of 'Rambo' kind of guy, he's got some fucked up boobie-traps up there, I've seen them firsthand, so don't stray too far off the main road."

Someone else spat. "What about if there are women up there?"

Donnelly's eyes narrowed. "You do what you feel is… necessary."

A silence passed through them. No one smiled. Power had just been handed over. And they were ready to wield it.

Toby stepped forward. "We're ready, Sheriff."

Engines ignited. Headlights surged forward.

Anthony's radio chirped alive, it was the channel for the "Holler Net". He answered and it was Ms. Maybell's voice, it came through in a low hiss. "Anthony, listen to me. Sheriff Donnelly just rolled through here with a convoy. Old trucks, side-by-sides, loaded down with armed men. He had Toby Willard with him, who if you don't know is really bad news— and he's deputized all those bastards. Says you're under arrest for murder."

Anthony's heart spiked, but his tone remained steel calm. "How many?"

"Four, maybe five trucks? At least a dozen armed men. They were braggin' about it like they were headed to a turkey shoot. They'll be on your road in five minutes, tops."

Without another word Anthony spun to face the others inside.

"We have incoming!" Anthony barked.

The room snapped still.

"Kill the lights—kill everything!" he shouted, flipping the master switch on the wall. The house instantly fell into darkness. Only the low red emergency LEDs lining the floors flickered to life.

"Get your nods!" Anthony ordered. Isabella, Cari, Michael, and Wade moved quickly, grabbing their gear.

"Isabella, Cari, Wade, you stay here, you are our eyes, Channel 3 for comms" said Anthony. Wade was about to object but saw the look in Anthony's eyes and knew, this was something different.

Anthony stepped into the foyer and issued a crisp command to the dogs: "Pass Auf!"

Ira and Branwen perked up, hackles half raised, trained, and waiting. Outside, the compound lights powered down in sequence, plunging all three tiers into blackness. The only sound was the soft hum of activated night vision gear and the shifting of boots on hardwood.

Wade clipped on her headset and whispered, "All nodes are dark. Thermal beacons are ready if needed."

Isabella stood by the main monitor, ready to switch surveillance to passive IR and thermal cameras.

Cari stood, watching, unable to be frightened but was unsure of the world surrounding her. Michael came to her, looked her in her eyes and said "You are going to be ok, stay here, watch, learn. We have practiced this as a family for this very event to happen."

Cari's mouth opened but no words came out. Michael reached up, pushed her chin to close her mouth and kissed her. Cari nodded grimly, her hand on the pistol Isabella had given her earlier. Michael chambered a round, silent. "Just breath," he said, then moved towards the other men in the room to discuss options.

Anthony's voice came low, deadly calm: "Positions. We don't shoot unless fired upon. But if they come past the second marker, that's the landing of the second tier, it's the area right after the last curve in the driveway, then we re-evaluate our firing policy."

Blackie walked outside to his SUV with Boone, both grabbing their kit bags and moved back into the house.

Anthony reached under his desk and pulled out a small, rugged Motorola APX6000 radio— an analog-only, no-AI capable device used for secure tactical communications. He attached a Motorola PMLN6828A throat mic with whisper PTT, renowned in military and SWAT circles and clipped on a compact EP1323QR Hawk lapel speaker-earpiece for clear reception.

He handed the fully rigged radio to Blackie.

"Here. We're all on Channel 3."

Blackie took it, weighing the device in his palm.

"Analog only?" he asked.

Anthony nodded. "No digital, no AI backdoors. This is just plain, old-school comms."

Blackie smiled—quiet, approving. "I like that. Keeps it clean."

Anthony flicked the ptt switch. "Channel 3—group. If you don't hear us, don't assume we're gone, and here is a IR chem-stick, pop it and wear it, we all have them on so we know who is who out there."

Blackie slung the radio and Chem-stick on his vest. The throaty hum of analog static seemed comforting in the dark.

Blackie set down his rifle and popped open a matte black Pelican case on the table. Inside sat a high-cut bump helmet outfitted with L3Harris AN/PVS-31A BNVDs—white phosphor, dual-tube night vision goggles, military-only issue.

Anthony raised an eyebrow. "Didn't know those were on the open market yet."

Blackie looked up and smiled slightly. "They're not."

Unknown to the group, the police chief was in his cruiser and on the way to the front gate.

Chapter 30: Collision Course

The police chief guided his cruiser slowly down the long gravel driveway, tires crunching over loose stone as the vehicle crept through the mountain's tight switchbacks. It was just past 3 a.m., and though the sun had yet to rise, a veil of silvery fog unfurled between the trees, curling like ghosts around the pines. One hand gripped the wheel; the other clutched his radio. Nothing but static. The silence on the line felt heavier than the predawn air.

As he neared the base of the driveway, the automated motion sensors lining the entryway flickered to life. With a quiet mechanical hum, the iron gate began to slide open. Each second dragged like a slow drumbeat.

Down the road, beams of headlights cut through the fog. A dozen of them. Pickup trucks with peeling paint, rusting side-by-sides, and at the front of the line, unmistakable—Sheriff Donnelly's cruiser.

The chief's face hardened.

He dropped the cruiser into drive and rolled forward, hoping to clear the gate threshold before the oncoming vehicles closed the distance. His intent was simple: slip outside and let the gate shut behind him, sealing out the convoy.

But he had misjudged.

Donnelly wasn't slowing down.

The sheriff's vehicle surged forward, its brush guard colliding with the front bumper of the police cruiser in a brutal crunch. Metal shrieked, glass cracked, and the cruiser bucked backward under the force. The chief fought the wheel, but the momentum carried him deeper into the gate's track.

The automated system stuttered and stopped—jammed halfway.

Smoke hissed from the hood of the cruiser. The chief threw it into park and reached for the door handle. Ahead of him, headlights flared brighter. The sheriff's makeshift militia was rolling in— engines rumbling, weapons visible, silhouettes shifting in the back of pickup beds.

And the gate remained frozen, gaping open like a wound.

In the main house, Isabella leaned in toward the monitor, brows drawn. "Chief's going down the hill. That's his cruiser."

Anthony joined her, scanning the feed. "What the hell is he doing?"

Cari stepped closer, voice tight. "Is that smoke, or just fog?"

Anthony moved quickly to the wall panel, toggling the security systems. "Damn. I forgot to disable the motion tripwire at the front gate."

Wade hovered behind him. "Can we override it?"

His fingers danced across the controls. "Too late."

They all stared as the gate slid open and the cruiser crawled through—only to be rammed seconds later by the oncoming sheriff. The impact reverberated faintly through the morning silence. On screen, the police cruiser buckled. Lights flickered. The gate jammed in its open position.

Boone's face turned grim. "They just breached."

Isabella's voice was flat. "The gate's stuck."

Cari stepped back. "Those trucks... those men... they're not law enforcement."

Anthony's jaw flexed. "No. They're predators."

Smoke curled from the hood of the damaged cruiser as the police chief stumbled out, clutching his shoulder. The crash had knocked the wind out of him. Across the short distance, Sheriff Donnelly emerged from his cruiser with the practiced arrogance of a man who had chosen violence.

"Stand down, Chief," Donnelly called out, his voice too casual for the moment. "You're outside Bryson's jurisdiction. This is county ground now."

The chief didn't flinch. "Your authority ended the moment you started deputizing criminals. I saw the video, Donnelly. You executed Dale. You slit Wyatt's throat."

Donnelly tilted his head, mock surprise creasing his face. "Is that right?" He turned to Toby, who stood beside one of the trucks grinning wide. "Well, I'll be damned. Looks like I'm under arrest."

Then Donnelly pulled his sidearm.

The first shot hit the chief square in the chest, spinning him back. The second carved through his shoulder. Blood sprayed across the crushed gate as the chief crumpled, half-hidden in the swirling mist. Holstering his weapon, Donnelly turned to his crew.

Now knowing that there was video of the Dale and Wyatt problem, everyone was now a loose end up at the Russo property, he said,

"Move that cruiser. Change of plan. We're clearing the whole damn place. Leave nothing breathing."

Inside the Russo house, silence gripped the room as the group watched the monitor.

Isabella's voice cracked. "He just shot him."

Cari turned away, tears welling. Wade stepped forward; jaw clenched. Anthony's fists were white-knuckled.

Boone leaned closer to the monitor. "That's a flatbed."

An old international harvester flatbed rolled into view, rusted and monstrous, its diesel engine snarling as it pushed the police cruiser out of the driveway like scrap metal. Men in truck beds hoisted rifles, the anticipation on their faces twisted.

Michael exhaled slowly. "That's not a posse. That's a warband."

Anthony's voice was low, edged in steel. "They chose this."

Cari wiped her eyes, nodding. "We're ready."

Through the fog outside, figures began to emerge, backlit by the hazy glow of halogen headlights. The compound's external sensors pinged softly.

"They'll hit the second marker in two minutes," Boone warned.

Anthony turned to the group, scanning each face. "Positions. Lights out. And may God forgive us for what's about to happen."

Chapter 31: Resistance Ignited

Anthony burst through the front door with Boone, Blackie, and Michael following close behind. The sharp bite of predawn air stung their faces as they moved with determination. Anthony pointed toward the top tier ridge, his breath puffing out in short bursts.

"Boone, Michael—take positions there and there," he said, gesturing with precision. "Eyes on the second tier bend. That's our kill zone."

Boots crunched across gravel and dead leaves as the team scattered. Anthony veered toward a steel pole embedded at the edge of the yard. Welded to it was a frame supporting four thick steel tubes, each mounted on swiveling hinges like the barrels of a war machine waiting to awaken.

Blackie paused, lowering his night vision goggles. Through the phosphorescent green hue, he watched Anthony remove weatherproof caps from the tubes with quick, practiced movements, absolutely filled with curiosity of what this crazy basterd was doing now.

Anthony keyed his throat mic. "Wade, prep tubes one through four. Fire at one-second intervals."

Inside the house, Wade sat before a makeshift command center— a custom-rigged MacBook Pro running an offline macOS, hardened against any AI interference. Multiple monitors displayed surveillance feeds, thermal sensors, and status readouts. Her fingers danced across a mechanical keyboard.

Wade selected the "Mortar" link in the command window options taking her to a screen with a perimeter view showing boxes with numbers in them that depicted the locations and numbers of tubes surrounding the top tier perimeter. The console was connected via a digital path to a FireFly fireworks launching system. "I'm in," she confirmed. "Launch sequence is primed."

Anthony adjusted the angle of the tubes, aligning them toward the bend on the second-tier drive.

Anthony gave the next order through his open radio channel. "NODS off."

Headlights appeared in the distance—ghostly and slow through the mist.

"Fire one," he said.

A whoosh echoed as the first tube discharged, launching a mortar that hissed through the air in a glowing arc. It bounced once on the gravel before detonating beneath the lead vehicle. A thunderous blast followed, blinding and deafening. The truck jerked violently, veering into a poplar tree, its front-end crumpling in smoke and steam.

"Fire two."

The next mortar screamed skyward, exploding overhead with a brilliant white flash. The second truck's driver stared upward— just in time to plow into the wreckage ahead. The impact launched two men from its bed into a rock wall. One crumpled lifeless; the other rolled in agony, blood soaking his clothes.

"Fire three."

The third projectile collided with an open-top Jeep, bursting in flames. The driver's screams rose as he clutched his burning arms.

"Fire four."

The final mortar landed just off-road, exploding with concussive force. Dirt and debris rained down on the last vehicle, the entire convoy halted in a choking cloud of fire and chaos.

Anthony gave the next order through clenched teeth. "Eyes closed until I say to open them, put your hands over them, tight….it's about to get bright."

Men below shouted, cried, and staggered in confusion. They weren't warriors. They were opportunists. Thugs.

"Wade—cue the track. 'Jungle.'"

Wade went back to the main menu, selected the "Music" tab, and selected all speakers and lights that lined the entrance road.

And with that, Russo territory declared itself.

The sheriff, bringing up the rear of the convoy, slammed his brakes as the pileup unfolded in front of him. Smoke, screams, and fire painted the scene in chaos. His men— convicted thugs and desperate locals— spilled from their trucks and side-by-sides, half-blind, half-terrified, stumbling toward the front.

Sheriff Donnelly leaned over the driver's seat, yanking his Remington 12-gauge from the rack.

A groan echoed through the trees as the tree hit by the runaway International Harvester truck finally gave way. With a crack like thunder, it fell atop the already clustered vehicles, its limbs shattering windshields and crumpling roofs like aluminum cans. Three trucks disappeared beneath the collapse.

Men screamed, some diving for cover, others running blindly as branches whipped down around them. The poplar tree's weight sealed off the bend.

Then came the sound.

Hidden PA speakers burst to life—200-watt screamers bolted high in tree trunks. From all directions, Axle Rose's voice exploded into the night.

The opening riff of "Welcome to the Jungle" by Guns n' Roses roared from the canopy, its grinding chords and chaotic tempo plunging the convoy into disarray. A few looked skyward, others scanned the tree line, mouths hanging open in confusion and panic. Then a female scream, raw and primal, tore through the speakers, cutting the air like a blade.

Before they could recover, the night exploded in light.

Four massive 1500-watt strobe panels— top-tier military-grade led banks mounted discreetly on trees— flared to life, flooding the clearing in a wash of blinding, pulsing white. Eyes already wide from fear were seared. Pupils slammed shut. Men dropped their weapons, staggered, fell to their knees clutching their faces. From a distance through the fog, the Russo compound lit up the holler like a music festival, minus the 120BPM music.

Psychological warfare at its finest—disorientation, overload, fear.

The strobes pulsed for five seconds—long enough to burn ghost images into the eyes of anyone looking up. Even in darkness, blinking lights echoed in the visual cortex like aftershocks. Panic spread like wildfire.

Then came the frequency.

A shrill, high-pitched tone screamed from the speakers—narrowband, high-gain, teeth-gritting audio that tore through the chaos like a scalpel to the brain.

Anthony's voice returned over the comms.

"NODS ON."

Anthony's voice cracked through the radio: "Engage."

With night vision goggles back in place, the defenders became ghosts in the pitch black. The moon had dipped below the ridge, and the night returned to darkness absolute.

From behind rocks, equipment piles, and barricades, the trained defenders of the Russo compound leveled their rifles.

The firefight was swift and brutal.

A one-sided slaughter.

With practiced precision, they fired bursts from suppressed rifles—5.56mm and .300 Blackout rounds ripping through soft targets below. Each shot dropped a man. The air filled with screams and the erratic staccato of poorly-aimed return fire from below.

Most of the sheriff's men were convicts and drunks, not soldiers. They fired wildly, some not even aiming, just squeezing triggers at flashes of movement they could barely see. They dove for cover, they screamed in fear. Men crumbled and fell into pools of their own blood and urine. Others looked on or just simply closed their eyes waiting for it to be over. Some ran for their lives.

Anthony coordinated fire through comms, calling out targets and cover zones.

Over the radio, Boone yelled he was hit.

"How" thought Anthony.

Blackie ran to Boone's position to help and protect. Boone was behind a stack of wood by a rock wall, still firing on targets as they presented themselves. Blackie ran up quick and startled Boone, causing him to draw down on Blackie. "What the fuck are you doing here?" Boone asked the man.

"You said you were hit, I had to see it for myself," he replied with a laugh. As he inspected the man, Boone pointed to his right leg. It was snapped out of place but not enough blood to show it was from a bullet. "What? Did you trip or something?" asked Blackie.

"No, fucking rock exploded from a fucking bullet from one of them assholes. It shattered the rock and it hit my leg, I think it chipped the bone or something, I can't put weight on it." Said Boone.

"Yeah, no shit, it looks like it shattered the femur. You NFL kicking days are over for sure," Blackie replied.

"Dick." Said Boone then winced in pain as he tried to reposition his kneeling position to fire on the enemy.

Blackie updated every one of Boones condition, nothing to be done right now but to fight.

Back near the bend, the sheriff had yet to round the corner. He stood between his vehicle and the corner, listening to the chaos unfold. One of his men bolted around the bend—bloodied and screaming.

The sheriff raised his shotgun.

"Get back up there!"

The man shook his head, panicked. "They've got fucking mortars, man! They've got NV—"

Boom.

The 12-gauge barked. The man's face disappeared in a mist of gore. Another two men rounded the bend at the same time as the trigger was pulled. They froze.

"If you're not with me, " the sheriff called, cocking the shotgun, "then you're against me."

He leveled the barrel. "Well? You with me?"

The two men exchanged a look, then slowly turned, and ran back uphill—until they noticed something.

A narrow dirt road veered off from the main driveway—an access point to the second-tier pasture.

They peeled off, disappearing down the side road.

Up in the command center, Isabella's motion sensors pinged.

"We've got two, tier two pasture road," she said into the mic.

Michael's voice came back. "I've got it. Send Ira."

"Raus, Ira," Isabella whispered. And told Cari to open the front door.

Michael moved with the quiet precision of a man who'd done this before— too many times. Each step along the rocky ledge of the second tier was deliberate, softened by instinct and the lessons of past patrols. Below him, the pasture was still, except for the barn Isabella had flagged— where she'd said she saw movement.

Through the green haze of his night vision goggles, the world sharpened into unnatural contrast. Two human silhouettes had broken from the main path, slipping into the old tier-two barn like shadows trying to outrun the night.

He gave a soft, two-tone whistle. Ten seconds later, Ira emerged from the darkness like a wraith. The Belgian Malinois crept up the incline, ears alert, muscles coiled, body low. He pressed against Michael's leg—silent acknowledgment of readiness.

Michael leaned down, voice barely audible. "Good boy." Then he pointed toward the barn, hand cutting through the dark like a blade. They moved as one— man and dog— descending in short, practiced bursts, navigating the twin retaining walls that marked the tier boundaries. Each four-foot wall was cleared in crouched steps, Michael pausing between them to listen. No voices. No movement. Just the distant pulse of small arms thuds from the ridgeline battle, echoing like some long-dead heartbeat through the mountains.

The last stretch of pasture was open ground—just over a hundred feet of exposed space, but they moved low and fast, slipping behind a wooden feeding trough warped by weather and time.

A moment later, the barn doors groaned on their hinges.

Two figures stepped into view, outlined in the fluorescent green of the NODs. Their heads were on a swivel, jerky, uncertain.

"I told you this was a stupid idea," one of them hissed. "We should've stayed low or gone back down. This place is booby-trapped as hell."

The other man's voice trembled, brittle and panicked. "You wanna go back through that hell storm? With that psycho sheriff? No thanks. Maybe we climb the back wall, flank 'em. Take the house from the side."

"We'll get lit up," the first man replied, glancing over his shoulder. "They've got eyes everywhere."

"Then we wait. Hide. Maybe they'll think we bailed."

But the conversation ended as one of them broke off, muttering under his breath. "Fuck this, man, I'm leavin'." He moved straight toward the feeding trough—toward Michael.

Michael breathed through his nose, slow and steady. He lifted two fingers, signaling Ira.

The dog sank even lower, all muscle and intent.

The man drew closer, his boot falls careless in the quiet grass. Twenty feet. Fifteen. Muttering something incoherent, close enough now that Michael could see the gleam of sweat on his temple.

He whispered one word.

"Zugreifen."

Ira exploded from cover in a blur of sinew and silent fury. The intruder barely had time to register movement before eighty pounds of trained violence hit him square in the chest. They crashed to the ground, a muffled grunt escaping before Ira's jaws found the man's throat. One savage shake, and a geyser of blood arced into the air. The scream that followed was short— cut off mid-throat, replaced by a wet, choking gasp as the man spasmed, then fell still.

Michael was already up, rifle shouldered, crosshairs locked on the second man.

Frozen. Mouth open. Eyes wide.

"No—!" the man managed to yell before the rifle thumped. A quiet cough of suppressed fire, but final all the same. The bullet struck center mass, staggering him backward. He dropped like a sack of grain, clutching at his chest, twitching, then going still.

Michael advanced with methodical caution, sweeping the area. Nothing else moved.

Ira stood panting over his kill, blood soaking his muzzle, the glow of the NODs casting his eyes in an eerie shimmer. The dog's chest rose and fell with intensity, but he remained alert, poised for another command.

"Clear," Michael murmured into the mic. "Two down. Tier two pasture secured."

He knelt beside Ira, fingers brushing the dog's neck in a firm pat. "Hell of a job." Then, with calm authority: "Auf deinen Platz." Telling the dog to return to home.

Ira hesitated, ears flicking. He pressed his snout into Michael's hand, unsure.

"Now," Michael said with finality.

The dog obeyed, bounding back across the pasture, then up the two low walls like they were mere curbs. He vanished into the upper tier shadows.

"He's on his way home," Michael called softly over the radio. Then added, "I'm moving to the main road to flank. IR beacon's hot— don't fricken shoot me." A dry chuckle followed, tension bleeding into the humor.

He turned, heading in the direction the two intruders had come from, each step measured and silent, the forest edge ahead steeped in shadow.

Behind him, the pasture returned to stillness—save for the bodies. Above, the mountain trembled again with the distant rhythm of gunfire. The war hadn't stopped. It had just passed over this tier... for now.

Chapter 32 – The Line Crossed

Michael silently made his way to where the access road met the main drive. To his right was where the men still fought, to his left was the way down the hill and the corner. Left side being clear, Michael slowly started his way upwards, the intruders not knowing he had completely flanked behind them. With precision, Michael called out his targets to the other men on the radio net and engaged. Without warning the war erupted behind the men and they started to fall from their relative safety. As they moved for new cover, they exposed themselves to the marksmen at the top of the ridge. Within seconds, the remaining threat was neutralized. Michael started sweeping the sides and noticed movement under the fallen tree, two figures moved in a low crawl with weapons, Michael crouched down and with two shots from his suppressed rifle dispatched both low crawlers. From the corner of his eye, he spotted two men run out of the back side of the tree and down the hill. With that he called up to the ridge that movement was no longer moving and two were fleeing down the hill.

Blackie and Anthony moved with urgency, but every step was measured, deliberate. The upper tier behind them still echoed with the chaos of the recent fight, but now the only sound was the soft crunch of boots over gravel and dirt. Their eyes swept left to right, searching every shadow and movement as they descended toward the lower level of the compound.

Michael stood from his crouch near the wood line. Dirt streaked his face, his shirt was torn at the shoulder where a ricochet had kissed the fabric, and blood had dried along one temple—but he was upright. Breathing. Alive.

"Hell of a mess, " Anthony muttered under his breath, rifle hanging low but ready, his gaze not leaving the tree line.

"I've got three wounded, two got away," Michael reported, his voice gravel-thick. "Six confirmed kills on this tier. At least six… that I've seen."

Anthony asked, "And the Sheriff?"

Across the courtyard, Cari and Wade sprinted to Boone's side. The old soldier sat propped up against a raised planter box, his face pale and drawn, one leg twisted unnaturally. Wade dropped to her knees beside him without hesitation, hands already moving with practiced focus.

Cari's voice cracked as she knelt opposite her. "Stay with me, dammit," she said, brushing sweat-soaked hair from her eyes.

"I'm alright, I'm not leaking anything." Boone rasped, his voice a dry whisper. "Pretty sure the leg's shattered."

Wade reached into the open first aid kit beside her and pulled out a collapsible splint. She didn't waste time. "This is gonna hurt you more than it hurts me," she muttered, a backward phrase that momentarily puzzled Boone— until her hands gripped his boot and shin.

With one swift, brutal motion, she brought the lower half of his leg into some vague semblance of straightness in an effort to ensure that the blood flow was not pinched inside the break. Boone let out a raw scream and collapsed sideways, fists pounding the dirt. Cari moved quickly to secure the splint as Wade held it in place, the two women working in grim silence while Boone groaned through clenched teeth.

Anthony took a step forward but froze. A sharp metallic click sliced through the air.

A hammer.

"Drop it," said a voice—low, mean, and loaded with malice.

Michael stiffened. Cold steel kissed the back of his neck.

"Easy now," the voice repeated, closer, full of threat.

The sheriff had moved quickly out of the tree line behind Michael where he placed his pistol to his neck. His uniform was torn and bloody, his face scratched, his eyes wild and burning. But he was alive—and seething.

"You sons of bitches," he hissed. "You think this is your turf? This is my county."

Anthony's eyes tracked the movement as the sheriff slid in behind Michael, using him as a shield. Too quick to intercept. Too close to risk a shot.

"Let him go," Anthony said, his voice calm but edged with iron.

"You drop yours first," the sheriff snarled. "Both of you. Or your boy here's gonna get ventilated. I ain't bluffin'. You think I won't?"

Anthony didn't move. Neither did Blackie.

The sheriff shifted slightly, making himself a harder target. He positioned Michael in front of him, only a sliver of his face and head visible over Michael's shoulder.

"You've got about five seconds," he spat. "One... two..."

It happened between heartbeats.

Blackie didn't telegraph the motion. One second his arms were at his sides, and the next the suppressed SOCOM .45 was in his hand. It moved like an extension of his body—smooth, fast, precise.

Phup.

A puff of white vapor hissed from the suppressor. A red mist blossomed from the center of the sheriff's forehead, just above the bridge of his nose.

Phup-Phup.

Two more rounds—tight, controlled—slammed into the sheriff's chest. His body crumpled behind Michael like a marionette with its strings cut, hitting the dirt in a lifeless heap.

Michael didn't move. Blood trickled down the back of his neck where the muzzle had pressed seconds earlier.

Anthony stepped forward slowly. "You alright?"

Michael blinked, the world around him slow to return. "Yeah... yeah. Just didn't expect that."

Blackie calmly re-holstered the weapon, as if the entire thing had been routine.

Anthony turned toward him, eyes narrowing. "Blackie... what the hell was that?"

"That piece of shit crossed a line," Blackie said flatly.

Michael exhaled hard. "Jesus. That was fast. I didn't even see it."

In the distance, faint but growing, came the keening wail of sirens—bouncing off the ridgelines, rising like a warning cry.

Anthony glanced toward the upper slope. "Second time in two days. Hell, the neighbors are gonna talk."

He turned back to Michael and Blackie. "Get eyes on that treeline. Those two who ran might come back. Let's finish this while we still can."

The compound shifted again—from the chaos of battle to the tension of aftermath.

And as the sirens closed in, so did the reckoning.

Down at the base of the mountain, where the gravel drive met the cracked county blacktop, a crowd had gathered.

Word had spread fast, as it always did in these hills—gunfire, smoke, something bad up at the Russo place. Again.

They came in pickup trucks and side-by-sides, on foot, and even horseback. Some wore sidearms and carried rifles across their backs. Others brought nothing but questions. At the center of it all stood Ms. Maybell, wrapped in her ever-present knitted shawl, her wiry frame anchored to the earth like weathered stone.

Near the stone pillars that marked the compound's entrance, a figure slumped against the rock wall. For a while, no one noticed him. But when the first responders arrived, they spotted the movement.

A side-by-side pulled to a stop. Two men jumped out and rushed to the fallen figure.

"Chief!" one of them shouted.

The man stirred, blinking slowly. His face was pale, blood soaked through the right sleeve of his uniform shirt, and his vest was torn at the shoulder strap. He groaned as he tried to sit up, using one arm for leverage.

"I ain't dead," he muttered. "Feels like I oughta be... but I ain't."

His left hand fumbled toward his chest, fingers brushing the shredded Kevlar where a slug had embedded.

"Stopped the first one," he rasped. "Second got me from the side. Sheriff Donnelly... goddamn lunatic."

"Help's comin'," one of the locals promised, steadying him.

Fifteen minutes later, the holler was full. Neighbors checked in, and the whisper of EMS coming through the gorge passed from person to person like prayer beads.

Then—more noise. Crashing steps. Branches snapping.

Two men burst from the brush, sprinting toward the gate. Their clothes were torn, faces cut, blood smeared down one arm. They looked like ghosts—wild-eyed, panting, but alive.

A dozen rifles leveled in their direction.

"Don't move!"

"Hands where we can see 'em!"

The two froze, breathing hard.

"We're not armed!" one of them shouted. "We were attacked—we didn't shoot anybody!"

A deep voice answered coolly. "Hit your knees."

Two men moved in from the line—one broad-shouldered with a buzzcut and a scar above his eye, the other lean, methodical.

Veterans both. Within seconds, they had the intruders disarmed, restrained, and face down in the gravel.

"They were part of the group," the chief mumbled, barely sitting upright now. "No doubt in my mind."

Ms. Maybell had pushed through the crowd and dropped to her knees beside him. Her joints popped, but she ignored the pain, brushing the graying hair from his forehead like a mother would a fevered child.

"You look like hammered shit," she said softly.

The chief gave a rattling chuckle that ended in a grimace. "Feel worse."

"Don't you go passing out now. You done been shot and lived—no point dying from embarrassment."

He managed a weak smile. "You always talk this much when a man's bleedin'?"

"Only when I care," she murmured, pressing her palm to his cheek. "You stay with me, honey. Help's just over the hill."

Around them, the community held the gate. Rifles ready. Questions unspoken. The line had been crossed.

And the war wasn't over yet.

Chapter 33 – Restoration or Reckoning

The first light of dawn crawled over the mountain ridge like a cautious scout, its golden fingers brushing the smoke-streaked remnants of what had been an invading force. Charred vehicles lay silent, their steel husks steaming, paint blistered and cracked. The smell of scorched rubber mingled with gunpowder and singed pine— a brutal perfume of battle freshly ended.

From deeper in the valley came new sounds—diesel engines groaning up the grade, the pulsing whine of distant sirens, and, above it all, the low rhythmic chop of rotor blades rolling across the sky like thunder wrapped in discipline.

The sheriff's remaining men had either fled into the thick woods or bled out on the gravel. Those who surrendered were cuffed and sat slumped against broken vehicles or tree stumps, eyes empty. The compound gates, still damaged and leaning from the earlier chaos, creaked open as the first wave of responders filtered in.

A battered county cruiser arrived first, its emergency lights flashing like a desperate heartbeat. Behind it came the only two deputies left on the payroll— grim-faced and shaken— escorting a young man with red-rimmed eyes and trembling hands. The sheriff's nephew stepped out slowly, arms raised, eyes scanning the carnage with disbelief. It was clear from his expression: this wasn't what he signed up for.

Over the ridge, two Bryson City patrol cars arrived, followed quickly by a pair of black-and-silver state police cruisers. They parked with practiced precision along the shoulder, officers stepping out with wariness in their posture. What they'd expected was unclear— but it hadn't been a battlefield.

Paramedics rushed to set up triage. The Swain County Fire Department brought chain saw crews and a crane team to clear the massive tree that had crushed half a dozen vehicles during the fight. Firefighters barked over radios and moved with urgency, cutting branches and guiding trucks into better positions.

Just inside the gate, where the grass was dark with blood, the wounded police chief leaned against the stump of an old oak. His uniform was soaked red from chest to hip, but his eyes remained sharp and clear, refusing to close.

The first officers to reach him dropped beside him, radios crackling. The chief winced as a medic peeled back his vest. "Sheriff Donnelly shot me," he rasped. "Shot Dale. Cut Wyatt's throat. Executed 'em. Deputized a bunch of thugs and tried to wipe out a family. The Russo's didn't fire first. They defended first."

A young state trooper crouched beside him and nodded grimly. "We've got drone footage. Partial feeds. It's bad. But you're safe now. EMS is stabilizing you."

Medics worked fast, cutting fabric, pressing gauze, checking vitals. One called for air evac, suspecting internal bleeding. Another tried to locate an exit wound.

The chief grabbed the trooper's sleeve. "You ID every one of those bastards. Some weren't local. This went deeper than Donnelly. He was just the tip of something bigger."

Up the mountain, Boone lay beneath a canopy of trees, sweat beading on his brow as two medics worked on his leg. A ricocheted chunk of stone had shattered the femur. He gritted his teeth and focused on the sky above, refusing morphine. Not yet.

Anthony stood nearby, his arms folded, scanning the scene with a soldier's clarity. Wade sat on the porch with Isabella slumped beside her, both too tired to speak. Blackie stood a few paces back, arms resting at his sides, but his eyes were still hunting— old habits didn't die easy.

Then came the sound that changed everything.

It started as a vibration, then grew into a thunderous whump-whump-whump that rolled over the trees and bent the branches. The UH-60 Black Hawk appeared just above the ridge, its matte black hull catching slivers of sunlight as it banked low across the compound. There were no insignias. No tail markings. Just war paint, a refuel boom arm, and intent.

The belly-mounted optics swiveled, scanning the compound, reading heat signatures and facial profiles. Leaves scattered in its downwash, and dust kicked up in heavy spirals.

Anthony shielded his eyes.

"Black Hawk," he said flatly. "That's not National Guard. Not federal."

Blackie squinted, then tilted his head. "I think that's for me, was a Night Stalker bird."

Anthony shot him a look that spoke volumes.

Blackie raised a hand. "Yeah, yeah… I know. I'll explain. Later."

The helicopter didn't land—just circled once, then banked north, vanishing into the lingering morning mist.

Michael appeared beside his father, breath shallow.

"You think they're coming back?"

Anthony's jaw tightened. He didn't answer at first—just stared after the departing bird, thoughts racing.

"Yeah," he finally said. "They're just waiting for a clear spot."

Crews went to work carving out a landing zone between the house and the barn. Trucks were backed out of the area and fuel drums relocated. Within five minutes, a 100-by-100-foot clearing had been opened up.

The Black Hawk returned—its blades slicing the air with surgical menace. The ground shook under its approach. Dust and shredded bark spiraled skyward as it flared, descended, and finally touched down with controlled violence.

The side door slid open with a metallic hiss.

A tall figure stepped out, ducking beneath the rotors. His uniform was starched and flawless, his hair silver and close-cropped. Two stars gleamed on his collar.

"Major General Sutherland. North Carolina National Guard," he said, extending a hand.

Anthony stepped forward. "Anthony Russo."

The General gave a small nod. "Figured as much. I've been sent to bring you to Raleigh. This isn't a request. Clive's there. Wants eyes on you personally."

Anthony's expression shifted. "Clive Simpson?"

The General didn't answer. He turned instead to Blackie.

"You Bravo-1-5?"

Blackie nodded once. "Affirmative."

"Thanks for the bird, now get on it." Sutherland said. "Convoy's inbound to secure the site. We'll lock it down. We've got cleanup and containment starting in thirty."

Blackie turned toward his SUV. "I've got a jet to catch I guess."

The General nodded. "RDU. You're headed for Site R."

Anthony frowned. "I can't leave. My family—"

"You're not being asked," Sutherland cut him off. "You've got ten minutes to pack. Three days minimum."

Wade stepped forward and wrapped her arms around Anthony. "Go," she whispered. "We'll hold the line."

Blackie retrieved his go-bag and a secure sat phone from the SUV. As he walked past Isabella, he stopped.

"You got a ride, kid?"

She shook her head.

He tossed her the keys. "She's yours now. Treat her better than I did."

Before she could answer, he turned. Gave Boone a thumbs-up, got one in return. Winked at Michael. Nodded at Wade and Cari. Then strode across the field like it was just another mission.

Anthony hugged Wade tightly, held her longer than usual. Then he met Michael's eyes.

"I've got this," Michael said simply.

Anthony nodded, crouched beside Ira and scratched behind his ears, then walked over to Boone.

"They're asking me to go," he said quietly. "I'll be back soon."

Boone grinned through the pain. "Don't keep the brass waiting."

Inside the house, Anthony grabbed his pack—three days' worth of clothes, essentials, and a journal tucked into the side pocket. Then he stepped back into the daylight and joined the General and Blackie. As they climbed aboard, the General waited for them to secure headsets. The rotors thundered above them, dust swirling like ghosts. The moment the green lights went live, he keyed his mic.

"Would one of you like to tell me what in the exact fuck just took place here?"

Blackie looked at Anthony. "I was here, and I'm still figuring that out. What was that Guns-N-Roses shit?"

Anthony laughed, "Saw it in a YOUTube video once, except it was with Roomba robot vacuums."

Blackie laughed so hard you could hear him over the rotor wash. "Well, we have about 45 minutes to RDU, please, tell us what the hell just happened"

Anthony leaned back, strapped in, and gave a tired smile.

"This is home," he said. "And it's everything I'm willing to fight for."

The Black Hawk lifted off, tilting north into the rising sun.

Below them, three armored Humvees rolled up the mountain road, .50 cals mounted and manned—another layer of protection settling into place around the Russo family stronghold.

The reckoning had passed.

But the restoration?

That was just beginning.

www.ingramcontent.com/pod-product-compliance
Lightning Source LLC
Chambersburg PA
CBHW020135120726
47903CB00007B/2264